A KIND OF ARMOUR

A KIND OF ARMOUR

Michael Humfrey

JOHN MURRAY

For Jackie, my wife

© Michael Humfrey 1985

First published 1985
by John Murray (Publishers) Ltd
50 Albemarle Street, London WIX 4BD

Typeset in 11/15 Baskerville Linotron 202
by Inforum Ltd, Portsmouth
Printed and bound in Great Britain
by The Pitman Press, Bath

British Library Cataloguing in Publication Data
Humfrey, Michael
A kind of armour.
I.   Title
823'.914[F]   PR6058.U39/
ISBN   0–7195–4198–0

Monday, June 19th

I left for the *cayo* this morning before sunrise, my eyes heavy lidded from lack of sleep. I had not shaved for three days; the stubble chafed the skin in the creases beneath my jaw and soured my temper. The tar-stained canoe which I had hired to take me to the island was moored at the foot of a frail wooden jetty. A hurricane lantern standing on the bow locker cast a soft-edged circle of light over the little vessel and the dark sea around it. In the wider darkness behind me, perched on its narrow spit of sand, the shuttered fishing village was still asleep. A dog barked once and was silent.

The two black fishermen in the canoe greeted me quietly; they were shivering a little in the early morning chill. The sweet, cloying scent of marijuana hung about them in the still air and I could see that the man crouched in the bows had already entered that good-natured, lethargic world of fantasy to which the drug grants access. His older companion had removed the spark plug from the outboard motor and in the pale glow of the lantern he was wiping it clean of oil on the tail of his shirt.

I was suddenly on edge, impatient to be gone.

'You should have done all that before I arrived,' I chided.

The man was not aggrieved. 'Is all right, baas,' he replied softly. 'We soon leave now.'

I climbed down from the jetty into the canoe and the man

in the bows left his place there and stowed my canvas bag and the small crate of tinned food on the floorboards of the vessel beneath my seat.

'We soon leave now, baas,' he echoed placatingly.

The man in the stern replaced the plug in the cylinder block. He stood up, wrapped a frayed length of cord around the spindle and pulled it out in one practised heave. The scarred, rust-stained engine burst at once into life, shattering the crystal stillness of the early morning. The other man cast off the rope which bound us to the jetty and the canoe glided swiftly away towards the narrow exit from the village harbour. Reflected on the glassy surface of the water the stern lanterns of a pair of fishing schooners, moored bow to stern in the deeper water of the channel, danced sedately in our wake.

The canoe passed out of the sheltered water of the harbour and the bows rose steeply to meet the first swell of the open sea. A burst of cold spray slapped me on the face, the salt crusting in my hair and stinging my eyes. The man in the bows had forgotten to secure the lantern. I saw it tremble on the oily cover of the locker and then pitch over the side. For a split second I could see the light shining upwards through the green water like the baleful eye of some submarine demon; then the hot glass mantle fell apart and the sea extinguished the flame.

The man in the stern cursed softly. 'Jesus Chris', man . . .' he complained above the clatter of the engine, raising the palms of his hands in despair. 'Why you can never remember to watch what you doin'?'

His guilty companion grinned sheepishly and threw overboard the glowing end of his marijuana cigarette. I could just make out the quick flash of white teeth in the black mask of his face.

'That is what happens when you people smoke ganga,' I said sharply.

'Yes, baas,' he agreed without rancour, 'sure, baas . . .'

'You have to forgive him, baas,' the older man said, raising his voice above the clamour of the exhaust and tapping his forehead with an oil-stained finger.

'You don't have to forgive anyone for anything,' I replied wearily, but I was thinking of Simone and I do not believe he heard me.

Behind us, silhouetted against a purple backdrop pierced by the stars and a misty three-quarter moon, the mountains of the Jamaican mainland receded into the darkness.

About an hour later, the sky began to lighten over the eastern horizon. I gripped the streaming gunwale with both hands and turned to watch the sun hoist itself above the rim of the sea in an explosion of scarlet splendour. A wedge-shaped cloud hanging over the water in the direction of Haiti glowed in the sky like a burning coal. At that very moment, somewhere beneath it on the streets of Port-au-Prince, I knew that the false brotherhood of the crippled and the starving would be making their way to the docks, jostling and kicking each other for the prime positions from which to display their deformities to the white tourists as they disembarked from their cruise ships later in the day.

On my own last visit to Haiti I had set up my easel on the waterfront determined to record the scene, but the express-

7

ions on those twisted black faces soon exposed the limits of my skill. I returned, chastened, to the less demanding seascapes of Cap Haitien and those panoramic views of Christophe's Citadel which I have always been able to sell successfully from my Jamaican studio.

The same sun that fell upon the distant Haitian misery gilded the white caps of the waves around us; the canoe pitched heavily in the rising swell. High above us, caught in the pure light of the morning which sharpened all outlines, a solitary frigate bird wheeled effortlessly in a wide arc across the sky.

The wind veered from the west. The man in the stern shut off the outboard motor and unfurled the patchwork sail from its bamboo mast. The urgent, unnatural clatter of the pock-marked engine was replaced by the music of the sea. The boom ran out, the sail filled with air and the canoe glided forward between the troughs in swift bursts of motion; I watched our wake carve an ephemeral path across the tumbled surface of the sea. The wind sang at the masthead. The blunt extremity of the outstretched boom dipped into the water at the bottom of each trough and rainbows formed in the dancing spray, dissolved and formed again.

The growing heat of the sun began to warm the old planks of the vessel. In the crevices along the sides the tar softened; it gleamed as black as the skin of the man at the tiller and the sour stench of countless generations of dead fish, impregnated forever in the rough surface of the planks, rose from the bruised wood. The man in the bows stirred softly in his drugged sleep but did not wake.

The warmth of the morning and the sea rhythm of the

8

canoe combined to cast their old spell upon me. I dozed fitfully, my back wedged against the foot of the mast. I had been sleeping for more than an hour when the man at the tiller woke me. He pointed to the east where the horizon was obscured by a thick curtain of rain cloud.

'You can see de *cayo* over dere, baas,' he said. 'De rain fallin' 'pon it now.'

As I looked in that direction the cloud began to lift and beneath it, balanced on the fine arc of the horizon, I saw the soft outline of the little island. The light of the sun was caught by a ribbon of golden sand and by raindrops on the palm fronds and on the leaves of the white cedar trees which cloaked the flat-topped hill in the centre of the island. The green cloak of trees was embroidered with bright tongues of scarlet flame wherever the stands of poinciana and immortelle were in flower. The *cayo* shimmered in its cobalt setting like some precious, verdant jewel. I stood up in the wet, heaving canoe, my arm clasped tight around the bamboo mast; it was more than thirty years since I had last seen that distinctive silhouette rising from the sea and my heart leapt with a sudden, unexpected surge of pleasure.

The man in the stern gripped the tiller between his knees and reached into the locker beneath his seat to fetch out a trolling line. He baited the hook with the dessicated body of a jack cravalle and tossed it overboard. The silver corpse of the fish planed over the water, dancing madly in the broken wake. The man paid out more line, passed it over a cleat on the gunwale and then looped the other end casually around his bare foot. Two bottle-nosed dolphins disdainfully inspected the bait then surfaced on either side of the canoe to

9

keep station just ahead of our bows; but in spite of the following wind we were moving too slowly for their taste and they soon made off towards the shipping lanes further south in search of larger, more substantial vessels.

Perched on the distant rim of the sea the *cayo* heaved itself further out of the water as we approached. Soon I could make out individual trees among the grey-green file of coconut palms which marked the upper margin of the beach and, not long afterwards, the foam-laced crescent of the coral reef which guarded the lagoon came into sight.

Above my head and level with the ragged birgee at the top of the mast a pair of brown pelicans were making for the *cayo* on the same stiff breeze that gave shape to our patchwork sail. Beneath the keel the rich, opaque blue of the open sea imperceptibly gave place to more subtle shades of lapis lazuli and translucent jade as the water shoaled. The wind backed a few points into the north; the helmsman adjusted the sail and the fragrance of the *cayo*, that unforgettable blend of fallen leaves and damp coral sand was borne down to us over the water. Instantly the scent of the little island brought back to me the bitter-sweet memories of my visits to the place when I was a boy.

The man at the tiller must have been watching my face.

'You been dere before, baas?' he asked.

'Yes,' I said. 'I used to spend time there with my father when I was young.'

He shook his head sadly. 'Well, you goin' see it haven't change at all. De place need brightenin' up before people goin' live dere. Maybe if dey put up a big hotel an' dredge de lagoon for a marina it wouldn' be too bad . . .'

10

I could see him painting in his head a picture of what it might look like with all the trees felled to make way for the hotel and the reef blown up to allow the big yachts to pass freely into the lagoon. The picture evidently pleased him, for where there were hotels there was a market for his fish.

We were closing the island fast and he put aside his thoughts about what might be to haul in his line. The head of the jack cravalle he had used as bait was still firmly attached to the hook, the barb protruding through the empty socket of one eye, but the silver body of the fish had gone. A jagged slash three inches behind the gill slits showed where a cunning barracuda, or perhaps a hungry lemon shark, had conjured the bait from the hook.

The man looked at the severed head of the cravalle without expression, removed it from the hook and tossed it overboard. We tacked twice to pass through the narrow passage in the reef which guarded the elliptical lagoon and glided swiftly across the still, protected water towards the beach. The man in the bows opened his eyes and shook himself free from the kindly grip of the marijuana in time to drop the sail; the keel of the canoe grounded lightly on the sand.

I kicked off my shoes and climbed over the side; my bare feet sank deep into the fine, wet sand. The men removed my modest luggage from the bottom of their canoe and stacked it neatly in the shade of an almond tree at the top of the beach.

The older man was suddenly concerned about me.

'Dis is one lonely place, baas,' he murmured. 'You sure you want us leave you here alone?'

'Yes,' I said firmly. 'I will expect you back in eight days.'

'O.K., baas,' the man replied. 'We goin' pick you up a week from tomorrow if dat is what you really want.'

I could see that he clearly thought that no one in his right mind would choose to spend eight days on a deserted *cayo* by himself, but he was too polite to say so.

I knew that both men were anxious to return to their village in daylight; they still had their fish traps to raise and their nets to haul.

'You better leave now,' I said. 'You will have the wind against you this time.'

The men nodded, raised their hands in a grave little salute of farewell and swung the bows of the canoe around to face the reef.

'Keep well, baas,' the man in the bows shouted and I watched from the beach as the sail was hauled up the mast and the canoe slipped easily through the passage in the reef and returned to the open sea.

The wind had veered again and quite soon the triangular outline of the patchwork sail merged with the white tops of the tumbling waves and I could no longer distinguish the little vessel from the sea around it.

I walked slowly up the beach to escape the heat of the sun in the shade of a coconut palm. Beneath it a tall pillar of coral, torn from the reef by the fury of some forgotten hurricane, sprang from the loose sand like the stump of a ruined Egyptian obelisk. I sat down with my back propped against the coral pillar. The trade wind was warm and comforting against my bare chest; the iodine scent of cast-up sargasso weed baking in the sun was heavy on the air.

I listened to the voice of the island: the bass murmur of the surf on the crescent reef, the seductive whisper of the breeze through the feathery palm fronds above my head; the scurrying passage of the iridescent ground lizards across the sand; the soft gasp of the waves expiring on the beach in front of me. I thought: the fisherman was right; nothing on the *cayo* has changed since I was last here; but there is not much left within me of that eager boy of thirty years ago whose life was still in front of him.

The voice of the island stirred old memories. From my seat against the coral pillar I looked down the length of the golden beach to where the sand reluctantly gave way to a low bulwark of limestone rock. I recalled a morning on my last visit with my father when I had discovered there a shallow rock pool abandoned by the retreating tide. Enchanted by the miniature world which lay beneath the crystal surface of the water I had knelt upon the sharp rock at the edge of the pool; there, screened by a loose fold of purple algae, staring up at me from the floor of the pool, lay the empty shell of a fallow deer cowry.

It was a thing of such improbable, delicate beauty that I scarcely dared hope that it might have survived intact its long journey from the deeper water where I knew it had once lived. But when I lifted it out of the pool and turned it over on the palm of my trembling hand I saw that it was undamaged, its exquisite enamel surface without the smallest blemish.

I do not know how long I remained squatting uncomfortably on the furrowed edge of the rock pool, the oval shell resting lightly in my hand, reluctant to break the spell of that enchanted moment. Surely, I remember thinking, in all the world there can be nothing more perfect than this porcelain miracle placed where I should find it by the sea; and suddenly I was certain that my life would be full of moments like that one and ahead of me wonderful things were in store.

A ragged bank of cloud passed over the sun and I was reminded that I would need to build myself a shelter to sleep in before nightfall. Not far from where I sprawled against the coral pillar the sea had carved a horseshoe indentation in the smooth sweep of the beach. A tangled pile of driftwood had collected there, cast high up on the sand by the last spring tide. There were pale, sun-bleached lengths of bamboo, old and brittle but still strong enough for my purpose; and among them lay a few splintered planks of wood with sparse traces of red and green paint which suggested that they might once have formed the side of a fishing schooner, victim perhaps of the same storm which had carried the pillar of coral across the breadth of the lagoon.

I lashed the driftwood together with a frayed length of rope which still clung to one of the planks and carried the bundle to a level plot of sand in the shade of a twisted almond tree. There I built myself a simple shelter with bamboo corner posts and a roof thatched with fallen coconut boughs.

When I had finished, I stood back some distance to admire my work. I had never built a shelter of that kind before and I was childishly pleased with the modest result. On the far side of the almond tree there was a poinciana in bloom. I broke off a cluster of the brilliant scarlet flowers and fixed them above the entrance to my shelter; but the cheerful effect did not suit my mood and I flung them away soon afterwards. I spread my sleeping bag on the dry sand floor within the shelter and stacked outside it the tins of food I had brought with me and a small sack of potatoes.

A coconut palm, its trunk bent double by some freak accident in its youth, grew close to my shelter. I used my sheath knife to cut loose one of the green nuts which clustered beneath its crown and opened it there on the sand. The sweet water was cool on my tongue. I sliced open the nut and scooped from within it the thick white jelly. Then I set out to climb the hill which rose in the centre of the little island and gave to the *cayo* that distinctive, shark-like silhouette.

There was no path to the summit through the bush and I soon discovered that I had forgotten the route which I used to take as a boy. I forced my way between stocky clumps of sea grape trees, carving a passage through the undergrowth where I could not thrust it aside. The slope of the hill was steeper than I remembered and the trade winds had sculpted the groves of white cedar into flat, impenetrable planes. Beneath my feet the soil was loose and lithic and each uncertain step sent little avalanches of stones chasing each other down the hillside.

It took me more than half an hour to reach the summit. At the very top there was a narrow platform of granite and, in shallow, earth-filled depressions which cratered the smooth face of the rock, rotund cactuses had taken root, their bulbous heads crowned with diadems of close-set purple flowers. I brushed carelessly against one of the fat green barrels and instantly four bright rivers of blood sprang from the muscle of my calf where a cluster of stiff needles had punctured the sweating skin. With some difficulty I cleared a place on the granite platform and sat down on the warm rock. I looked out over the feathery crowns of the coconut palms and the tall almond tree which concealed my shelter, and upon the golden ribbon of sand where I had stepped ashore from the canoe; and once again I felt the force of that old enchantment which the beauty of the island had always laid upon me, its seductive magic undimmed by the passage of time.

On Admiralty charts of the northern Caribbean the *cayo* hangs like a tear-shaped jewel from the fine thread of the eighteenth parallel. In total area it can be no larger than a pair of football fields, but there is level ground only at the eastern extremity of the island, the flattened head of the shark silhouette. From my granite platform I overlooked both the windward and leeward shores, the latter steep and broken like some nightmare lunar landscape, defended from the onslaught of the waves by a rampart of granite boulders which have fallen from the overhanging cliff above them.

On calm days the sound of the sea is little more than a whisper here: the muffled slap of wave against rock; the quiet chuckle of water flowing into a thousand secret channels; the sibilance of air expanding under pressure through some narrow fissure in the face of the cliff. But there are other days at the beginning of each year, when the trade winds capture the sea far out in the eastern Atlantic and hustle it across the empty ocean, and the impact of each towering wave shakes the island to the roots of its granite foundations. There is a perpetual roar like the thunder of some distant cataract and the windward shore is shrouded day and night in a writhing blanket of salt-laden spray.

The sheltered leeward side of the *cayo* is a different world.

There are no boulders here, no massive rock defences to resist the attack of the waves. The golden beach is open and vulnerable, protected only by the arms of the coral reef which reach out to enclose the lagoon. To my artist's eye the colours of the sand are the soft colours of 18th-century France, cream, rose madder and buff; and everywhere along the line of the last highwater there are windblown hillocks of sea shells, glowing in the sunlight with brighter, more obtrusive colours.

On the windward shore, where deep water closes the island, the sea reflects the sapphire blue of the West Indian sky; here, on the other side, where the shallows extend far out beyond the beach, the crystal water is amber and jade green, changing in intensity with each subtle, cloud-induced variation of the light.

Up there on the summit of the *cayo*, I did not feel the discomfort of the unyielding rock; I thought only: I am in harmony with everything about this island. I was right to come back . . .

I must have fallen asleep there on the hilltop, because when I next looked out to sea again the sun had already slipped beneath the arc of the horizon. Directly below me, the alchemy of the evening light had transmuted the blue water of the lagoon to beaten silver. High above the western horizon a single, unremarkable cloud hung in the sky; but as I watched from my hilltop, its untidy mass was touched by the fingers of the Midas sun. The thin, pale streamers which hung beneath it were washed with gold; above them, the heart of the cloud seethed with scarlet fire.

The brilliant colours gave way to softer, pastel hues and

17

then the darkness came down all in one piece like a shutter. Beneath the undergrowth around my granite platform the first creatures of the night stirred at the end of their twelve hours sleep. I shivered a little in the evening chill, conscious that I wore no shirt, and made my way cautiously through the little minefield of barrel cactuses down the steep slope of the hill the way I had come.

I was tired by the time I reached my shelter. I had eaten nothing since early morning. By the light of a hurricane lantern I put together a simple stone hearth beside my shelter and lit a driftwood fire. The familiar smell of frying sausages mingled with the sharper scent of burning bamboo logs and drifted up among the palm trees with a pale grey smoke.

Afterwards, in the veiled light of the stars, I sat on a sand bank at the top of the beach, a mug of coffee in my hand; except for the soft fall of the waves and the song of a cicada in the almond tree behind me, there was silence.

The three-quarter moon rose above the horizon and laid a dazzling path of light towards me over the surface of the sea. The silver ribbon of the beach stretched away in the distance to merge with the shadow of the limestone platform in which I had found my fallow deer cowry all those years ago. Beneath the sea grape trees on either side the fireflies glowed like aerial lighthouses in the darkness. A desperate unhappiness settled over me.

I moved back to my shelter and crawled inside. The strident song of the cicada faltered and then ceased as the love-sick male found his mate. A cloud passed over the face of the moon and the fire in the hearth died out.

I slept fitfully beneath my palm-thatched roof.

Tuesday, June 20th

I woke this morning at sunrise, my body bathed in sweat. I had been dreaming of Simone. In the dream I saw her wandering naked along the beach, searching for me among the sea grape trees which grow close to the water's edge.

'Michael, where are you?' she kept repeating; and then I was walking beside her on the sand. She put out her hand to touch me but there was a wall of ice between us, as sheer and green in the sunlight as the side of a glacier.

'Forgive me,' I heard her whisper, 'forgive me.' But I turned away from her and walked slowly up the beach until I entered a forest of close-set, misshapen coconut palms which seemed to stretch away into the far distance for ever. Behind me, as I passed, the trees bent down towards each other, barring all possibility of my return that way.

I had noticed that her cheeks were wet with tears, but when I sat up in my driftwood shelter to shake myself free of the dream I discovered that the tears were my own.

I lay back on the sand. In the fading light of the stars outside, all along the margin of the night's high water, an army of nocturnal hermit crabs were scavenging for whatever they could find. The crabs made a soft metallic sound as they hauled their shells among the flotsam; apart from that curious noise and the ceaseless murmur of surf upon the reef the island was wrapped in silence.

19

I crawled out of my shelter into the pale light of dawn. It must have rained a little during the night for the sand outside was damp beneath the soles of my bare feet. I noted with satisfaction that the rain had not penetrated the thatched roof of my shelter. I lit the fire in the stone hearth and brewed some coffee; I drank it black without sugar and the nightmare world of the dream began to relax its hold upon me.

I wandered down to the edge of the water. The high tide had raised a bank of sand along the beach during the night and I sat there on the sand to watch the sun rise over the horizon. Within the inflected arms of the reef the surface of the lagoon looked as if some skilful glazier had capped it with a single sheet of glass. Out beyond the reef, the breast of the open sea breathed lightly, rising and falling with the gentle movement of the underlying swell.

The sun rose in its extravagant tropical beauty. I stopped shivering as it dispersed the morning chill. High above the summit of the island, above the granite platform and the barrel cactuses, a wisp of cloud was set on fire by the sun; the perfect scarlet image of the cloud seemed to hang in the depths of the lagoon beneath the cap of glass, the immaculate reflection more beautiful than the cloud itself.

With the enamel mug of coffee still clasped in my hand, I walked down the beach towards the limestone outcrop which contained the rock pool. Ahead of me a strutting group of sandpipers tossed the flotsam at the water's edge. As I approached, they turned to face the sea and took refuge in flight, their plaintive, high-pitched call of alarm echoing across the lagoon.

I gazed down the length of the beach, divided now by its

tide line of brown sargasso weed, and at once the scene brought back to me the image of my wife in my dream last night and the cold hard wall of ice which had stood between us.

'Michael, where are you?' she had cried. Where indeed, I thought as I wandered on towards the end of the beach.

I can remember every detail of the letter; I recall with perfect clarity the texture of the paper, the exact colour of the ink, the bold, confident style of the writing. Looking back on it now, I believe that in a curious way even before I read the words I knew that they were going to shatter the foundations of my comfortable world.

It was Saturday afternoon. Simone was playing tennis at the time. I had returned the previous day after a week in Haiti. I was in my studio fitting a stretcher to one of my paintings of Sans Souci, Christophe's ruined palace in the north of the country. It was a view of the onion-domed palace chapel together with the stone sentry boxes and the massive entrance gates which stood beside it.

There was an overlap of canvas at one end, but I could not find the knife I needed to trim it. I left my studio and walked across the hall into our bedroom to fetch a pair of scissors which Simone kept on her dressing table beneath the mirror. The scissors were not in their usual place; I opened the narrow drawer in which she stored her reels of cotton. The letter lay beneath them, its crisp edges almost hidden by the bright cylinders of colour. I hesitated for a long moment, unwilling to concede that between us there might be anything but perfect trust.

From the yard at the back of the house the voices of our old cook's grandchildren drifted through the open window. It had not rained for several weeks and the fine red dust which discoloured the lawns rose in lazy, spiral clouds when it was disturbed by the children's feet. In my studio the colours of my finished canvases were becoming muted by a thin film of dust which stubbornly resisted every effort to remove it. I remember thinking: I must tell old cook to keep them off the grass. They can play in the paddock if they like.

Then I shook the letter from its envelope.

'Every night before I fall asleep,' he had written, 'I kiss the place where your body lay beside mine. I think of the sweet velvet of your breasts and the touch of your thighs beneath me . . . I remember how you cried out each time we reached together that special place that only lovers reach . . . I remember how you hungered to be loved . . .'

For a long moment I felt nothing; my mind refused to accept the meaning of the words I read. I thought quite calmly: he writes well this man; he chooses his words with care. Then a giant, implacable hand grasped my stomach, turning it in upon itself, squeezing, wrenching, tearing, forcing it up against the muscles of my diaphragm until I groaned in agony upon the bed.

When the spasm passed I lay there on the bed, a blanket of darkness and despair wrapped close about me, the letter crushed savagely between the palms of both hands as if, by an effort of will, I could wring out of it those cyanic words as one wrings water from a flannel. On the reluctant screen of my mind appeared the first images of the two of them together. I saw her naked on his bed, her long legs spread wide for him. I saw them coupled on the bed, that firm, ripe, suntanned body that I knew so well moving slowly with him to that same peak of ecstasy she always sought to scale with me. In my imagination I heard the familiar, triumphant cry that signalled her release.

She had returned home not long afterwards to find me sprawled upon the bed, the letter still clasped between my fingers, the careless laughter of the old cook's grandchildren still echoing across the yard behind the house.

She grasped at once what had happened. She stood there in the doorway, casually beautiful in her white tennis shorts and thin silk blouse, her fingers clenching and unclenching around the handle of her racket, her face chalk white in the fading evening light.

'Oh, dear God,' she whispered, the words catching in her throat, the tears flooding at the corners of her eyes. 'Oh, my darling, I never meant to hurt you.'

I put the letter down on the bed and she came over and stood close beside me. I could feel her body trembling against my shoulder. She stretched out her hand to touch my cheek in a hopeless gesture to stem the pain. I heard her whimper again, softly like a frightened child: 'I never meant to hurt you.'

'How many times?' I asked.

There was a long moment of silence in the room.

'I must know how many.'

'I don't know,' she said helplessly. 'Can it matter all that much? Seven, eight . . . I don't know. It just seemed to happen sometimes when you were away from me in Haiti.'

'Where?' I demanded, and the beat of my heart seemed to fill the whole room.

'Oh, darling,' she pleaded, 'does it really matter now?'

'Yes,' I said.

'On the beach, in a hotel, in his house, once in this room . . .'

'In our bed?' I asked incredulously. 'Here, where we make love?'

She nodded miserably.

I got off the bed and walked over to the window; at the far corners of the parched and dusty lawn purple shadows had gathered beneath the poinciana trees. I saw that the brilliant colours of the climbing bougainvillaea were already muted by the failing light.

She came up silently behind me and wrapped her arms about my waist in that familiar gesture of love which often in the past had brought a swift end to petty disagreements. She rested her cheek against my back and I could feel the wetness of her tears seeping through the thin stuff of my shirt. Her breasts were soft and full against my spine.

'I love you,' she whispered. 'I never loved him. I only love you.'

'Then why did you do it?' I asked, in a voice I scarcely recognised as my own.

I felt her body tremble against mine.

'Why?' I asked again. 'Why, if you love me?'

There was another long moment of silence between us. She released me and sat down upon the bed. She looked up at me, her eyes rimmed with scarlet, her cheeks wet with tears.

'Why do you find it so hard to tell me that you love me?'

24

she asked, answering my question with a question of her own, her voice barely audible above the distant murmur of the traffic on the road beyond the lawn. 'Why must you always fence off part of yourself from me, as if I was a stranger instead of your wife?'

She reached out for my hand, but I stepped backwards to the window again.

'Is it so wrong for me to want to hear you say you love me?' she asked.

I said nothing, my unseeing gaze fixed on a pale rectangle of empty sky above the guango tree that marked the boundary of my land.

'You wear a kind of armour round your heart,' she said. 'I knew it was there when I married you, but I thought in time my love could melt it away. I was wrong. I can not penetrate it.'

'What could he give you that I can't?' I demanded, not choosing to answer her questions.

'He gave me love,' she said. 'He loved me and he told me so. He never hid his feelings.'

She stood up and took my hand and held it against her breasts.

'I need to be told,' she whispered. 'I just need to be told.'

In the brick-red dust of the back yard the children were playing still; the bright sound of their laughter was cut short at last by their grandmother's sharp command to come inside. Beyond the lawn the tops of the casuarina trees seemed to sway drunkenly towards each other in the gathering darkness. I clutched at the window ledge to prevent myself falling.

'Forgive me,' she whispered again; but I turned away from her so that she should not see my face. Wrapping about me the ragged cloak of my pride I fled from the room.

I had left my car at the front of the house. We had planned to go out to dinner that night. The keys were still in my pocket. I drove like a madman through the warp and the woof of the traffic on the coastal highway, turned to put the sea at my back and climbed the steep, tortuous road into the hills.

I arrived at a clearing near the highest point of the road and swung the car on to the hard mud surface. A thin mist veiled the floor of the valley immediately beneath me and far beyond the valley, as I watched, the lights of the little groups of houses strung out along the coast came on one by one. The amber pinpoints shimmered like stars through the thin curtain of mist.

On one side of the clearing there was a grove of mango trees; the sickly-sweet stench of the fallen fruit was heavy on the air. The mountains all around me, from which I had always drawn such pleasure, loomed grim and forbidding now, their furrowed peaks starkly silhouetted against the pale evening sky.

I thought: it is all over and I have got to get away. I cannot bear to be near her now; I cannot face the awkward sympathy of friends. I must set a distance between myself and every other human being until new skin has had a chance to close the wound. I have got to adjust to life without her.

I knew that, if I stayed, there might well be another ending to the story. One night in the weeks that lay ahead when I could not sleep, and when heart-ache and self pity had drawn the sinews out of me, I might be tempted to get into the car and drive up there again; and this time when I turned on to the clearing by the mango trees my hand might not reach instinctively for the brake and I might let the car carry me nine hundred feet down the hillside and into the mist-shrouded bed of the ravine at the foot of the valley, to the last inviolable sanctuary.

I did not want to end my life in that way.

I remembered a man I had once known, a fellow artist, who was himself confronted with a situation not so very different from my own. He told me how he had faced up to the same urgent, insidious desire to escape forever from his grief. He had fought it, he told me, by giving form in his imagination to that siren song of self-destruction. He had conceived the temptation as a marauding tiger, hungry for his life. In that way he gave substance to what was otherwise only a dark shadow with which he could never really hope to come to grips.

Eventually, with the passing of the years, he had seen off his tiger. He gathered around himself the fragments of his life and even contrived, from time to time, to milk a degree of contentment from his reduced existence.

'We are all going to be a long time in the grave,' he said to me. 'It is foolish, when you think of it, to add even one unnecessary minute to that eternity.'

Now I was confronted by a tiger of my own with its breath hot against my throat. And it was at that moment, sitting there in the car with the distant lights of other people's houses winking at me through the evening mist, that I remembered the lonely *cayo* I used to visit with my father long ago. I thought: I will go there and face my tiger on that battleground.

In the event, it was not difficult to arrange.

I returned to my palm-thatched shelter, stoked the smouldering embers of the fire in the hearth and tossed three strips of bacon into the frying pan; but the rich, clean smell did not entice me. I ate without appetite or enjoyment.

When I had finished, I threw sand on the fire and climbed the long slope which led up to the edge of the cliff that overlooked the broken windward shore. I sat down there on the succulent grass which curled over the lip of the granite cliff like a green moustache and watched the great white-capped rollers drive in towards the *cayo* from the east.

As the morning grew older, the wind rose; soon it was tearing the spray from the tops of the waves as they reared up like prancing stallions to assault the ramparts at the base of the cliff. The wind hurled the spray up the glistening face of the cliff in ragged sheets of vapour. Warm salt caked thick upon my lips; spray stung my eyes and cheeks like spent shot.

I took shelter behind a weather-scarred boulder at the top of the slope. I lay on my back in the lee of the boulder, cushioned by the damp grass, and looked up at the bright bowl of the sky. Above me, an endless succession of rainbows formed and disolved in the flying spray, their ephemeral colours set against a constant sapphire background. The wind howled around my boulder. The beauty of the morning banished the tiger from my presence and I wished with all my heart that the moment might never end.

I climbed down from the edge of the cliff early in the afternoon and opened a tin of sausages. There is a breadfruit tree at the base of the slope and I roasted one of the heavy green fruit in the smouldering ash of the fire. Tomorrow I must begin to live off what I can catch in the sea. It is a long time since I had to use a spear gun to secure my meals.

I have brought a hammock with me to the *cayo* and after my meal I slung it between two coconut palms at the upper margin of the beach. The trade wind was warm against my body, the voice of the surf soft and seductive. I closed my eyes; but instantly cast upon the screen of my imagination appeared the image of my wife. She was on our bed at home, lying flat upon her stomach, her long, suntanned legs spread wide so that I could see the sweet pinkness there in the secret cleft of her body. I felt my heart race and the muscles of my throat constrict and I was suddenly consumed with a fierce, unendurable longing for her.

The wind breathed through the palm fronds around me and on the sand beneath my hammock a pair of pugnacious ground lizards charged each other with mock ferocity to affirm their claims to chosen strips of territory. Not far from where I had slung the hammock a ripe coconut broke loose from its high mooring and crashed down upon the sand. The lizards abandoned their mannered posturing and fled for cover. I thought: another man has taken her on that same bed; those long legs have closed around another man. What must they have thought of me when they were joined together on my bed?

My bloodied pride rose choking in my throat like black bile. With a desperate effort of will I forced the image from

29

my mind. I let the voice of the surf roll over me until at last I dozed fitfully in the hammock beneath the palm trees.

The sun had fallen to the horizon when I woke. Drugged by sleep, I could not recall where I was. The embers of the fire over which I had cooked my last meal gave up a thin plume of smoke and the acrid fragrance of smouldering bamboo carried me back down the corridor of the years to one of my earliest memories.

I was a child on my father's estate. It was early in the morning and in the field near our house a gang of black labourers were preparing their first meal of the day before setting off to work. Their deep, musical voices drifted over the stream which skirted the bottom of our garden, borne towards the house on the soft morning breeze with the smoke of their cooking fire. The men had carried with them into the field a portable grindstone. It was set up on a level piece of ground at the edge of the field and beside it stood a calabash and an old kerosene tin full of water. In the grey light of the dawn they took it in turns to sharpen their cutlasses against the stone.

There was a rhythmic creaking of the steel axle in its pitch pine cradle as the handles of the grindstone were turned around. A man threw a little water from the calabash on to the revolving stone and applied to it the edge of his blade; a high pitched, metallic shriek rang out over the field as the edge of the blade was drawn swiftly across the spinning stone.

I remember crawling out of bed to sit by the open window and watch the blue sparks leap from the tortured steel.

Mixed with the smoke from the cooking fire there was a sulphureous stench of hot metal and wet stone. My parents were still asleep and the servants in their freshly starched white aprons had not yet left the kitchen. The house echoed with a silence which would soon be disturbed by the morning routine of making it ready to face another day. I sat there at my window, deep happiness in my soul, requiring no more of life than life had given me, never doubting for one moment that it would always be so.

As evening fell over the *cayo* I climbed out of the hammock and walked unsteadily down to the water's edge to wash the skeins of sleep from my mind. At the far end of the beach a narrow bar of sand had been uncovered by the tide. A steel-blue heron stood motionless on the bar, the matchstick legs and crested head silhouetted against the bright light on the water behind it.

As I watched, a river of silver sprats flowed past the heron on their way to catch up with the retreating tide. The long neck arched and struck forward like a hammer; a shower of spray caught the last rays of the sun. A struggling silver body gleamed in the heron's beak; the long neck straightened, the crested head was thrown back and then the little fish was gone.

The shoal of sprats took to panic-stricken flight. I saw two or three fish, their sense of direction over-ridden by the common fear, drive up on to the beach. The heron left the water with purposeful, stiff-legged strides to pick them off the sand. The bird's tall reflection trembled on the water as the first breath of the off-shore breeze pleated the satin surface.

31

I walked to the end of the beach and then across the pitted platform of rock to the southern extremity of the *cayo*. A narrow U-shaped inlet thrust its way into the smooth curve of the limestone shore and a cluster of stilt-legged mangroves formed a dense screen at the water's edge. I hauled myself on to the arched buttresses of the roots beneath the canopy of leaves. If was like stepping into a church on a hot summer's day, with the branches of the mangroves meeting in a high Gothic ceiling above my head. A cool green light replaced the white glare outside.

I looked down through the network of rust-red roots. Within the lagoon the colours of the sea were the clean hues of sunlight; but here in the water among the mangrove roots, where the sun never penetrated, there were more sombre tones. Black and deep purple predominated, and on the surface of the mud I could see the soft sheen of mother of pearl in the scattered valves of dead mussels and tree oyster shells.

All around me pendant, tear-shaped seedlings hung down towards the water. As I brushed against one it broke off and fell into the sea. The ebbing tide bore it away, perhaps to form another colony of mangroves on some distant, uncharted bank of sand. Scarlet tree crabs retreated higher into the branches, menacing me with their open claws.

I swung myself out of the green light and back on to the pitted limestone at the edge of the inlet. Above the western horizon a thick band of cloud had gathered and the setting sun touched the base of the cloud with fingers of gold. I sat there on the sharp-edged rock and watched the brilliant colours fade to silver grey. A flight of pelicans, their crops heavy with fish, circled the lagoon to land on the water in their careless, clumsy fashion. Darkness came down over the *cayo* and the sea around it.

'Where do the colours go at night?' I once asked Christiana, my Haitian nurse.

'Dey go home to Massa God,' she said. 'He use dem to paint de sky nex' mornin'.'

'Why can't he leave them up there?' I had wanted to know.

'*Doudou*, you better ask him when you see him,' she replied, and I remember how her deep, throaty laughter filled my bedroom.

But it was the bitter-sweet sunsets of my childhood, and the yearning somehow to capture and possess those astonishing colours, that persuaded me to reproduce them for myself with paint and paper. For better or for worse I became an artist because of them; and yet the subtle light and the exquisite fusion of one bright colour with another elude me still.

I was not hungry this evening. The stew which I prepared over the driftwood fire did not tempt me. I forced myself to eat a few spoonfuls and then I emptied the pan beneath the almond tree where the root-ribbed sand was cratered with the holes of the ponderous land crabs.

I had taken a private oath that I would not seek solace in drink while I was on the *cayo*; but this evening I uncorked the bottle of brandy I had brought with me and I lay down on the sand at the upper limit of the beach. The pliant, sun-warmed sand moulded itself to the contours of my back, reluctantly giving up the heat it had accumulated during the long day. The evening breeze died away with the light.

I looked out across the water towards the white laced shadow of the reef. On the surface of the lagoon phosphorescent streamers of pale fire were born, lingered for a moment and then faded into the darkness as a pair of predatory houndfish hunted among the schooling sprats. From time to time a brighter cascade of light betrayed the presence out there of a large fish, a barracuda perhaps or a marauding hammerhead shark, and the uneven submarine battle in which the strong always prevail took a more violent turn.

The raw brandy set the back of my throat on fire and a dull contentment crept slowly up my spine.

The moon rose early, unfolding a quivering path of light across the water towards the place where I lay on the sand. In my imagination I struggled to my feet and hurried down the golden path towards the source of the light and a new world where there was room only for happiness and peace of mind; but on the watery track a step behind me I heard the soft tread of the tiger. I tried to run but my shackled feet broke through the polished surface and then I was in the water, powerless to raise my hands from my sides, and I knew that I was going to drown . . .

I smacked the cork into the neck of the bottle with the heel of my hand and flung the brandy out of reach on the soft sand behind me.

The moon dipped beneath a bank of cloud and low on the western horizon there was a faint blush of light. As I watched, the pale glow intensified and then separated into a hundred pinpoints of yellow light, like a distant, rectangular constellation. The lights moved slowly along the rim of the horizon and I realised that I was looking at a passenger liner, hull up on the edge of the sea. The vessel was travelling eastwards, bound for San Juan and Charlotte Amalie.

It was not so long ago, I thought, that Simone and I were passengers on a vessel just like that one, cruising south down the chain of the Antilles on our way to the carnival in Port of Spain. It was a holiday to celebrate our wedding anniversary and perhaps we had travelled on the very same ship. Out there, I thought, beneath the masthead lights, the cocktail bars will be full of the sound of laughter and the rattle of ice in tall glasses; and on the dance floor there will be pretty women in low-cut dresses and a band in braided uniforms. And perhaps in the darkness on deck, pressed against the ship's rail in quiet corners, staring out into the blank face of the night, there will be a few solitary men like myself, wrapped in bitter memories, wrestling with voracious tigers of their own. There are some on every ship; I had seen them when I was with Simone, and had pitied them in the detached way one pities beggars in the street. Now I was one of them, a paid-up member of that injured fraternity.

The wind rose, rustling the fronds of the coconut palms all around me, causing the shadows to dance upon the sand. Across the several miles of water which separated me from the bright lights of the cruise ship, borne over the sea by a freak gust of wind, came the sound of the band playing an old-fashioned waltz.

I cupped my hands to my ears to catch and amplify the faint echo; then the wind shifted and there was only the familiar song of the surf on the crescent reef. But the damage had been done. Somewhere, in some deep recess of my memory, those half-heard bars of melody, that beguiling combination of violin and piano and tenor saxophone, opened the floodgates and the tiger was at my throat again. The renewed longing for Simone seemed to break over me like a monstrous, towering wave, sweeping away the little cocoon of false contentment I had so laboriously constructed about myself with the aid of the brandy.

'Sheer off, you bloody ship,' I shouted into the darkness; and obediently, soon afterwards, the constellation of the vessel's lights began to fade once more into the soft pink glow I had first seen; then this, too, was extinguished as the hull of the vessel slipped beneath the horizon.

'Why can't you open your heart to me?' she had asked.

I crawled into my shelter, like a wounded animal seeking the comfort of its lair; or, perhaps, I thought, like a damaged child returning to the womb which had once protected it from hurt.

Merciful sleep closed around me, and all night kept the tiger at bay.

Wednesday, June 21st

I woke this morning at first light and stumbled down to the edge of the water to wash the sleep from my eyes. The salt stung the mosaic of mosquito bites which tattooed my forearms. I stood there with the sea lapping at my bare feet and looked down the length of the beach towards the limestone platform. For a moment I thought I must still be dreaming: in a broad band between the water and the upper limit of the night's high tide the ribbon of golden sand was flushed with purple. Then I saw the cause of it.

During the night, while I slept within my shelter, a colony of delicate purple sea snails drifting through the Windward Passage on the surface of the water had been blown ashore by a change in the direction of the wind. As the tide receded towards dawn, the little floating molluscs had been stranded on the beach. In their extremity they had used their one defence against disaster: they had stained the sand around them with the purple fluid from their bodies.

There must have been ten thousand of them and all along the beach an army of pale ghost crabs had emerged from their holes in the sand and were already sidling with grim purpose among the snails. Still drugged with sleep, I was suddenly enraged by the meaningless loss of life. A kind of madness held me in its grip. Nothing in the world was so important at that moment as the return of the shipwrecked molluscs to their proper element.

I knelt upon the damp sand, frantically scooping up in the palms of my hands as many of the fragile creatures as they could hold. Repeatedly I waded chest deep into the water to release them there upon the surface where they belonged. But the task was hopeless. The south-easterly wind, which had driven the snails ashore, was still pushing the water of the lagoon towards the beach. As fast as I returned them to the sea the waves carried them back one by one, stranding them for a second time, lacerating their delicate tissues and stripping away their rafts of air and mucus. After a while I saw that I was only serving to prolong the moment of their death. I gave up.

I stood there gasping for breath in the soft light of the dawn, surveying the beach with its pale purple margin and that vast, pathetic shipwreck of snails, outraged by the wasteful cruelty of it all. It was the element of mindless chance that offended me. If the wind last night had blown two points further from the east, I thought, or if ten million years ago the *cayo* had thrust itself to the surface only half a mile further west, then the colony of snails would have drifted by unharmed, safe to live out the full term of their brief lives. Instead, blind chance decreed that they should meet a cruel death on the island, either at the claws of the ghost crabs or in the dessicating heat of the morning sun.

But as I walked back to my shelter through the coconut palms the mood passed; my unreasoning fury melted away. The crabs have to eat, I reflected, and it was in the nature of things that other creatures must die so they can live. Perhaps my anger was because the purple sea snails were such

38

exquisite, blameless little shells and the sight of that mass death served to remind me that life is a lottery, without purpose and easily extinguished, my own no less than any other.

For breakfast this morning I ate the last of the bacon. Already it had begun to curl a little at the edges and the fat was rancid. Afterwards I made a brief inspection of the store of tinned food which I had laid out on the sand beside my shelter. It was not as I had left it.

I had arranged the small stock of tins in two neat rows, their labels to the front. Sometime during the night, however, my larder had been assaulted by the nocturnal land crabs, those giant grey relatives of the ghost crabs on the beach, whose gaping holes cratered the smooth surface of the sand beneath every coconut palm. The voracious crabs, with their undiscriminating palates, had eaten the labels from the tins and so, from this day on, I shall have no way of knowing in advance what I am likely to find when I open one of them.

I rearranged my tins in a defensive circle, as the settlers disposed their covered wagons to protect them from marauding Indians, and I placed in the centre of the circle those tins which still retained some fragment of their original labels. Then I took my mask, snorkel and spear gun from the canvas bag and carried them down to the end of the beach where the golden crescent of sand gave place to the platform of limestone rock.

Although it was still early in the morning, the sun was already raising shimmering waves of heat above the sand; when I turned to look back at my shelter the distorted trunks of the coconut palms were writhing like snakes at the top of the beach. I waded into the sea, slipped the mask over my face and bit down on the mouthpiece of the snorkel. The green water closed over my head, warm and protective.

The white sand which carpeted the floor of the lagoon stretched away in the distance towards the looming rampart of the reef. The trembling shadows of the ripples on the surface danced across the sea floor. I swam slowly out towards the reef, my own shadow, masked like some cosmic time traveller, creeping just ahead of me over the green meadows of eel grass which chequered the floor of the lagoon. Scattered colonies of fat white sea urchins grazed upon the blades of eel grass, their tests feebly camouflaged with the valves of dead venus clams and ragged fragments of turquoise sea lettuce.

Directly beneath me, the disordered shape of an octopus stalked warily across the intervals of sand. I filled my lungs with air, arched my body and sank down through the water. Clasped tightly in one of its tentacles, the octopus held a white clam. The intelligent, ice-cold eyes took careful note of me as I approached; then the mollusc turned its siphon in my direction and with an unexpected burst of speed propelled itself across the sand to a bed of eel grass where it sought the safety of its hole within the matrix of the bed. Widely scattered around the entrance to its lair was the evidence of countless excursions across the floor of the lagoon: broad-based pyramids of empty snail shells and their porcelain opercula, and the separate valves of several generations of white clams.

Beneath me the sea floor began to slope gently upwards

40

and the first stands of elk-horn coral, outposts of the reef which rose like a city wall in the distance behind them, thrust their branches towards the surface. My approach was greeted by a submarine chorus of clicks and groans and high-pitched whistles which increased in intensity as I drew closer. The metropolis of the reef, that warren of shadowy crevices and soaring coral towers, was alerting itself to the threat of my arrival.

The wall of the reef was encrusted with leathery mats of sponge in vivid shades of yellow and deep purple. Sponges of other shapes thrust their porous arms towards the surface and between each block of coral the lavender tentacles of giant sea anemones swept the water in a gentle, constant rhythm.

On the convoluted surface of each rounded mass of brain coral there were scattered colonies of flower worms. Their delicate filigree gills were arranged in twin spirals like Christmas trees. As my intrusive shadow passed over them, the little red and yellow gill plumes were folded shut like wet umbrellas and hauled down into their tunnels within the living coral.

A shoal of scarlet flamefish drifted along the coral wall with the current, their progress interrupted from time to time by the furious charges of the resident damselfish whose territory they innocently violated on the way. A pair of queen angelfish admired their reflections in the glass window of my mask.

Reluctantly I turned my attention to the task which had brought me to the reef. I moved along the face of the coral wall, searching for the secret hiding places in its cratered

41

surface. Thirty feet beneath me, protruding from a crevice where the base of the reef met the sand, I saw a pair of brown antennae. They were spurred like the trailers of a climbing rose and they swept the water from side to side in a gentle, elliptical motion.

I propped the butt of the speargun against the inside of my thigh and drew back the rubber thongs. They clicked softly into position and I slipped forward the red metal safety catch. I filled my lungs with the warm morning air and kicked my way down to the base of the reef, approaching the crevice well away from the coral wall so that my shadow should not fall across it. The pressure of the water clamped the rubber mask to my face and the familiar diver's song rang in my ears. I flattened my body against the floor of the lagoon.

The lobster was at peace within his refuge, sleeping perhaps after a long night digging molluscs from among the roots of the eel grass beds over which I had passed. The delicate antennae idly swept the water; my approach was too silent, too stealthy to cause alarm. Only at the last moment did the dark shadow of my body rearing up in front of him spark the instinct to take cover; and by then it was too late.

I squeezed the trigger of my speargun; the long steel arrow with the barbed head leapt away from me, the stout cord and its attendant train of silver bubbles streaming out behind like the tail of a comet. The lobster reacted at the moment of release, springing sideways in his shelter for the safety of a deeper passage in the coral; instead of striking the creature in the head where I had aimed, the arrow penetrated the carapace through the side of the thin-shelled thorax. At once the powerful tail lashed the water all around it. A thick grey

42

cloud of sand and coral debris rose from the floor of the crevice and hid the lobster from my view. The cord attached to the steel arrow was drawn taut as a bow string.

I braced my feet against the wall of the reef and heaved on the cord, but the wounded lobster resisted the pull of the arrow in its flesh and my lungs began to cry out for air. For a long moment the contest was evenly balanced; then quite suddenly the lobster gave in. I hauled in the cord, hand over hand, and as the creature was drawn through the mouth of its crevice I heard it cry.

It was an eerie sound, high-pitched, despairing, infinitely piteous. It was a cry I had heard before in the days when I spear fished every morning along the reefs near my Jamaican home, but it had never distressed me in the past. Shutting my ears to the sound, I gave one final heave on the cord. The lobster was hauled defenceless into the open water where there was no solid surface against which it could brace its body to resist the pull of the cord. I saw that the steel arrow had passed right through the lightly armoured body, the cruel barb protruding from the far side of the thorax.

I kicked up hard towards the surface, my lungs bursting, scarlet flashes clouding my sight. Far above me I could see the hard blue undersurface of the water, impossibly distant. I remember thinking: have I left it too late? It was a long time since I had dived so deep and the passage of the years had marked me. Then my head broke through and I drew the sweet air into my lungs, retching and gasping in the brilliant sunlight. I turned towards the beach, my heart beating like a trip hammer, the lobster strung out behind me like a kite on its cord.

43

The return journey, back over the scattered green meadows of eel grass, took a long time. Once, in the very centre of the lagoon, I glanced behind me and through the crystal water I could make out the torpedo shape of a marauding barracuda, attracted by the scent of the lobster's blood and the vibrations of its lashing tail. I turned on my back and brought both feet down hard across the surface of the water. Startled by the unfamiliar noise the big fish circled me once and then made off towards the passage in the reef.

My feet grounded on the sand. I struggled ashore and hauled the lobster up the beach. It lay there on the hot, dry sand, vanquished, its life oozing from the ragged holes on either side of its shell, the pale pink blood clotting on the sand around it.

I looked at the creature's long spider's legs, the broad segmented abdomen, the splayed tail, the two sharp spines which arched above the yellow match stalk eyes. Dragged up from its natural element, crushed by its own weight upon the sand, it was an ugly beast; but I had also known it at home upon the reef, powerful, graceful, as light on its long legs as a boxer in the ring. And now the creature was dying, drowning in the still air of the beach, melting in the fierce heat of the sun; and I had done it.

I lifted the dying lobster off the sand, extracted the steel arrow from his side and boiled him over the fire in the hearth. In spite of the gaping wound he did not die easily and the memory of his death agony was fresh in my mind as I separated the white meat from the shell.

I climbed into my hammock after the meal and, perhaps because I had not boiled the rich flesh long enough over the driftwood fire, my sleep was invaded by dreams. In them I was confronted by the lobster, swollen now to twice my own size with eyes as large as footballs. We were facing each other once again within the cramped tunnel of the crevice beneath the reef and the creature had pinned me to the coral wall with the tips of his antennae.

'Why did you do it?' he demanded. 'You must tell me why.' And in the curious way of nightmares, his voice was my voice.

Held fast against the rough side of the crevice, I was overcome by an unbearable sorrow: the creature could not understand that he had caused his own misfortune.

'Forgive me,' I pleaded. 'I never meant to hurt you, but you brought it on yourself.'

It seemed he could not hear me, for he kept repeating the question.

'Forgive me,' I begged again, but this time the water rushed in to fill my lungs.

'No,' I heard him say, 'Never.'

'Why not?' I gasped.

'The *houngan* told me to be hard,' he replied. 'I never forgive.'

The underwater scene wavered and dissolved, and when it formed again the lobster had become myself and pinned against the coral wall was the body of my wife, a bright silver arrow between her breasts.

I woke up then, curled like a foetus in the womb of my hammock, the sweat pouring in rivulets down the side of my face, conscious that I had shouted out in terror in my sleep and that a small flock of grey-winged plovers feeding at the

45

water's edge had taken to the air in fright. In the smoke-stained pot beside the hearth were the remains of my meal. I swung myself out of the hammock and buried the splintered fragments of lobster shell deep in the sand at the edge of the clearing.

I was overwhelmed by a desperate need for the touch of my wife. It was so urgent and so intense that in the lengthening shadows beneath the palm trees I knelt upon the sand and shut my eyes as tightly as I could to conjure up the image of her naked body. I had not done that thing for more than twenty years, but my hand had not forgotten how. There was a brief moment of sterile ecstasy and then that distantly remembered sense of anti-climactic release.

Like Onan's, my seed spilled upon the ground. I crept back to the hammock and this time I slept a sleep without dreams.

I woke when the sun was low in the sky, setting fire to a broad band of cloud which hovered over the rim of the horizon. My throat was bone dry and there was a bitter taste on my tongue. I sliced open a green coconut and quenched my thirst with the cool, sweet water: then I walked through the grove of palm trees and stepped on to the loose sand at the top of the beach. The sun had burned all day in a sapphire sky and the sand was like red-hot ash against the soft skin of my instep. I cried out with the swift, unexpected pain and leapt across the beach to the water's edge. On the surface of the sea a sudden gust of wind shattered the long mirror of the sun's reflection into a thousand golden fragments. I wandered aimlessly along the beach towards the

46

limestone platform at its far end, dragging my feet through the cool green water.

The early afternoon's high tide had carved a shallow depression in the sand mid-way along the beach while I was sleeping in my hammock. Into this narrow basin had been swept an untidy carpet of broken coral and empty coquina shells. The double valves of the little clams were spread open on the sand where they lay like a flight of exquisite porcelain butterflies. One of them was tiger striped with alternate rays of black and orange. I bent down to place it on the palm of my hand; beneath it, lodged between two pleated fragments of coral, I saw a large pink pearl.

Once before, when I was a small boy, I had found a pearl of this kind. I was walking the black sand beach of our estate and the pearl was wedged in the aperture of a whelk shell which had been flung far up above the high-water mark by some recent storm.

With a sharpened twig I prised the pearl from the grip of the shell and washed it clean in the sea. It had been chipped and abraded by the sand and the side exposed to the sun had been robbed of its deep, rich colour; but at that moment the world could have offered me nothing for which I would have exchanged it. I wrapped the pearl in a green almond leaf and dropped it into the pocket of my khaki shorts; then I raced back through the fields of ripe bananas to our house, my heart beating with an almost unbearable happiness.

When I reached the front steps, however, I discovered that there was a hole in my pocket and the pearl had gone. In the days which followed I scoured that narrow path which led between the banana fields until I could recall in my sleep

47

the shape and size of every pebble set in its dry mud surface. In the evening of the second day I found the withered almond leaf at the side of the track, but not the pink pearl I had placed inside it.

The pearl lying now at my feet on the *cayo* was no sun-bleached, storm-damaged jewel, however. This one had not been robbed of its beauty by the action of the waves which had swept it up from the bottom and brought it to my hand. The powder-soft sand had cradled it gently on its long journey across the floor of the lagoon from the place near the reef where the Queen Conch which fashioned it had lived and died.

I placed it in the hollow of my hand. In the soft light of the evening it glowed there on my palm with a pale pink fire. My fingers closed acquisitively around its satin surface; but quite suddenly, the desire to own the pearl, to possess its beauty forever, subsided and then died. I thought: this time I shall take nothing away with me; I shall leave it all exactly as I found it; I shall not rob the *cayo* of a single grain of sand.

I knelt down again by the side of the depression in the sand and replaced the pearl between the pleated coral fragments where I had found it. I walked on slowly down the length of the beach intending to make my way round the island to the windward shore before the light failed. But the old magic of the sunset laid its familiar spell upon me and at the end of the beach I halted to watch the ritual painting of the sky above the western horizon.

On the sand beside me a ground lizard extended the tawny membrane at its throat; beyond it, a pale ghost crab emerged from its hole to test the evening breeze. Apart from

48

the soft gasp of the waves on the sand and the cry of a returning sea gull there was silence.

I sat down on the trunk of a fallen coconut palm and at that moment, from somewhere above and behind me, the silence was broken by the sweet-melancholy call of a mountain whistler. The shy bird's song rang out in a series of clear whistles in phrases of two or three crystal notes, dropping more than an octave on the scale. The granite cliffs caught and amplified the sound so that I was unable to tell exactly where it came from. I listened for several minutes, entranced by the song, not daring to turn around in case I startled the singing bird and caused the flow of song to cease.

From somewhere among the cedar trees at the base of the cliff there was a report like a pistol shot as a dead branch snapped in the cooling air. The tide of music ceased, cut off in mid-phrase. I turned swiftly and caught a glimpse of ragged, dull-brown feathers against the lighter backdrop of the cliff. The silence flowed back and I thought how like this paradoxical world it was that a sound so enchanting should issue from the throat of so plain a bird.

Crouched upon a ledge cut deep into the granite cliff a green iguana basked in the heat which radiated from the smooth rock face. The big lizard was pressed flat against the rock; its saffron eyes looked down at me without fear.

There had been a cliff not far from our estate house and when I was a boy a large family of iguanas lived in the scrub around its base. Sometimes in the evenings I used to ride my donkey to the place to watch the iguanas crawl lazily out along the ledges to enjoy the last of the sunlight. In time they grew used to my quiet presence beneath them and I was able

49

to approach close to where they lived.

One evening the youngest member of the family took up position on the highest of the ledges when a chicken hawk made a slow pass across the face of the cliff. I knew at once that the hawk had seen the lizard and I watched it wheel across the sky to return from the opposite direction. I thrust my hands under the carpet of leaves around me, frantically searching for a stick of some kind, but there was nothing there but damp humus. Panic-stricken, I reached for the only solid object I could find, the treasured silver pocket knife clipped to my belt. As the hawk stooped towards the narrow ledge I hurled the knife upwards, the bright blade glittering in the fading sunlight; but with a contemptuous adjustment of its wingtips the hawk avoided the knife and plucked the young iguana from the cliff face as delicately as a girl might pluck a ripe grape from the vine. Like the lizard, my knife was lost forever.

Two days later one of the estate Overseers brought down the murderous hawk with his shotgun. The bird had been troubling a herd of goats with new-born kids and the Overseer had waited patiently all afternoon with his gun across his knees until the hawk's hunger overcame his natural caution and he flew into range.

The Overseer had carried the dead bird up to our house and proudly laid it out upon the cobbled apron in front of the stables, spreading the wings so we could better appreciate their span. Then he took from his pocket his curved pruning knife, that badge of office carried by every Overseer on the estate, and severed the legs. He exposed the white tendons and, manipulating them with his fingers, demonstrated on my wrist how the razor-sharp talons closed about the neck of their prey.

That night, with the kerosene lamp in my bedroom casting long, leering shadows on the wooden walls, I felt the scaly talons close around my own neck. In a feverish sweat, I had sprung out of bed and slammed shut the hurricane shutters over my window.

On the *cayo* the sun sank beneath the horizon and I watched the green iguana shake himself like a dog, crawl back along the ledge the way he had come and drop lightly into the undergrowth at the side of the cliff.

The colours in the western sky lost their fierce brilliance and I returned along the water's edge to my shelter beneath the almond tree. As I passed the depression in the sand, I noticed in the failing light that the tide was coming in and that the waves had already reclaimed the flight of porcelain coquina clams and the pink pearl which I had found among them.

I brewed myself coffee, black and scalding, and lay down on the sand beside the fire. The moon had not yet risen but already the familiar voices of the night were echoing all around me. Somewhere in the branches of the almond tree above my head a cicada began his serenade, like a shrill green violin stuck forever on the same falsetto note.

Beyond the grove of coconut palms there is a giant silk cotton tree, anchored to the soil of the *cayo* with roots which have withstood every hurricane for the past three hundred years. Its massive branches are bearded with shapeless

51

epiphytes and white tree orchids. In the watery microworlds where the branches join the trunk the tree frogs launched themselves into their own whistling melodies of love sought and love fulfilled.

As I lay there on the sand beside the fire, I did not find it hard to believe, as the aboriginal Indians believed, that each island has a soul of its own. I put my ear to the still-warm sand; the giant shadows of the trees danced in the light of the dying fire and I could hear the erratic beating of a granite heart in time with the rhythm of the surf on the reef which guarded the lagoon.

The island was alive; the trade winds breathing through the needles of the casuarina trees at the foot of the hill gave a gentle, hypnotic quality to its voice. The voice was warm and treacherous. 'Forgive her,' it whispered speciously, 'the fault was yours, forgive her. . .'

With a vigorous effort I broke out of the clinging web of sleep.

'No,' I heard myself shout, 'No, no, no . . .' The sound of my voice passed through the grove of palm trees; the echo was returned by the granite face of the cliff behind them. A startled nightjar resting on the sand flew up into the darkness. As the silence flowed back I could plainly hear the drumming of my heart. After a while I closed my eyes; my last conscious thought was: I'm glad I left the pearl there on the sand where it belongs.

I slept where I lay in the open beside my shelter and the light drizzle that fell upon the island did not wake me later in the night.

Thursday, June 22nd

I was woken this morning by the harsh rasp of the inter-twined branches of a pair of casuarina trees, driven against each other by the trade wind which had freshened during the night.

When I was a boy on our estate, there had been a grove of tall bamboo overhanging the stream which flowed around the bottom of the rose garden not far from the window of my bedroom. At night the east wind, which came off the sea heavy with salt and moisture, crushed the hollow bamboo stems against each other until the whole grove moaned and whimpered like a beaten child. Once, after a specially stormy night, I had confided my fear to one of our black cooks and the foolish old woman informed me that it was the spirits of damned slaves trapped in the bamboo that cried out so in the night; what I heard were the pitiful prayers of the spirits to be released from their purgatory.

For several days I had brooded unhappily over this news, unwilling to risk the sharp-tongued ridicule of Christiana by confessing my fear to her. At last I ran to my mother. I have never forgotten her anger. The old cook was banished at once from the house to take her place in the fields with the common labourers. Then, late in the afternoon of that same day, my mother had led me by the hand to the banks of the stream and together we sat on the sun-warmed grass, my hand in hers, waiting for the wind to rise and bend the bamboo stems against each other.

The air that afternoon was still, however. In the polished surface of the stream I watched the water boatmen skate over the dark reflection of my face. I listened to the muted, hypnotic song of the flowing water and smelt the sweet scent of the wild jasmine. The gravel bed of the stream was laced with the cobweb tracks of the crayfish which had fled to the shelter of the overhanging bank when my shadow fell across them. I picked up a broken twig and flung it into the water. It circled briefly in an eddy; then the swift current swept it between two sandstone rocks and bore it off to the sea.

Lulled by the music of the stream I fell asleep there on its banks. The breeze arrived at sunset and I was woken up to witness for myself how the green stems of the bamboo chafed against each other and so gave out that eerie, rasping sound. Wherever else they might be, it was clear that the souls of the unhappy slaves were not resident in the bamboo grove.

'You see,' said my mother, 'there is nothing more to it than that.'

I interceded for the old cook. 'Let her come back,' I begged. 'She really believes what she told me.'

My mother was implacable. 'No,' she said. 'There are some things in this world for which there can be no forgiveness,' and so the woman continued to labour in the fields.

But life, which so delights in irony, was to take those harsh words and fashion them into a sword with the cruellest of double edges; and in the fullness of time it was to cut us all to the bone.

My mother loved people and parties; all my most vivid memories of her are in some way bound up with her preparations for going out to dinner or for entertaining friends at home.

Every afternoon, or so it seemed to me, Janice her mulatto maid spread out upon her bed a selection of evening dresses and my mother would call me to her room to help with the problem of deciding what to wear that night. They were elegant, colourful dresses and they lay across the counterpane like fallen rainbows. The delicate fragrance of her perfume clung to them and conjured up for me bright images of my mother surrounded by a coterie of admirers, the centre of attention wherever she might go.

'What do you think of this one, darling?' she would ask, holding up the dresses one by one against her body as she admired her slim figure in the full-length mirror on the wall behind me.

'Yes,' I would say, eager to please, to make plain my devotion to her, 'I like that one and that one; I like them all.' And it was the truth, because we both loved the same combination of subtle colour and rich material, and she knew instinctively what clothes showed her figure to best advantage.

In due course Christiana would come to the bedroom door to collect me and I would be borne off to supper and then to bed. I used to see my mother again briefly when she came to my room to hold me in her arms and to kiss me goodnight. Her kiss was of necessity light as the touch of a butterfly's wing for her lipstick, so artfully applied, was not to be smudged.

With her mass of coiled black hair and her dark gypsy eyes, my mother was a most striking woman; everyone who knew her remarked upon it. How could I not have worshipped her when she dressed like an angel every night and smelt like the honeysuckle that scaled the walls of my bedroom and wrapped itself around the wooden hurricane shutters? When I think of her now, more than thirty years later, it is always that gowned and silver-slippered image that springs at once to mind.

My life revolved around my mother; she was at the very heart of my existence. Between us there grew up a special bond of love, strengthened no doubt by the fact that I was an only child and did not often meet other children of my own age. As I grew older and developed that sense of pure delight in the beauty of the natural world, a delight which time served only to enhance, she was there to share my pleasure and to applaud my attempts to capture it with crayons and watercolours.

'The thing about you and me', she once said, 'is that when we look we see *all* the colours of this world.'

My mother understood. I could no more have imagined my existence without her than I could my own death.

High up on the slopes of the Blue Mountains, tucked away among the pleated valleys, there was a small coffee estate with a holiday cottage which my father had bought as a wedding present for my mother. The clapboard building clung precariously to the mountainside, propped up in front by four thin mahogany pillars which gave it a curious, predatory aspect. We spent three weeks in the holiday cottage during the hottest part of each Jamaican summer and for as far back as I can remember we were always accompanied by a thin, bearded man I knew simply as Marcus. Marcus managed one of the small sugar estates which bordered our own property by the sea and I think my father felt sorry for him because, unlike us, he could afford no land of his own and had to be content with cultivating someone else's soil. He was a widower whose wife had died not long after their marriage, and the tragedy had left its mark upon him; but he was a kind and gentle soul and although he appeared shy and awkward in my father's company, I noticed that he could always find something amusing to say when he was alone with my mother and me. He once agreed to sit still for more than an hour while I painted his portrait and said kind things about the smudged result which I presented to him afterwards. I liked him.

It was cold on the slopes of the mountain at night. As the evening light began to fade, the brass oil lamps were lit and the servants closed the jalousie windows and prepared a cedar log fire in the living room. A sense of isolation from the real world, which stopped at the foot of the mountains, crept over us all with the darkness.

When I leapt out of bed in the morning, I would find the stilt-legged house wrapped in a blanket of mist. The thin, disembodied chatter of the labourers gathering for work in the valley below drifted up through the mist like voices from another age. The mist clung tenaciously to the dripping branches of the silk cotton trees and curled about the attenuated pillars which supported the front verandah; and in the stillness which flowed back after the men and women had scattered to their various tasks, the melancholy call of the grey-winged mountain doves echoed across the unseen floor of the valley.

The rising sun dispersed the mist. At one moment the house would be securely cocooned in its damp white blanket; then, without warning, a shaft of light would pierce the gloom and instantly the mist would be drawn up the side of the mountain to rest all day like a housemaid's cap upon the very summit.

In the evening, I would walk with my father through the fields of coffee which surrounded the house and sometimes we pressed on into the fringe of the trackless forest beyond the borders of our land. On our way through the fields we often met the gangs of labourers trudging back in the soft evening light to their huts in the valleys below. As my father and I approached, they scuttled to the side of the path and waited respectfully, caps in hand, for us to pass by.

'Evenin' baas,' they chorused, 'evenin' young Massa,' and my father would return their greetings and occasionally inquire perfunctorily about the health of their families. He used a severe tone of voice when he addressed his black employees, 'just to make sure they remember who's who' as he put it. And if the dutiful smiles of his labourers were a little too wide and were not reflected in their dark eyes, he never appeared to notice it.

Marcus did not come with us on those evening walks; apparently he felt obliged to stay behind to keep my mother company. On one occasion, when rain swept across the side of the mountain and caught us on the track, my father and I returned unexpectedly to the cottage. I remember thinking that both Marcus and my mother looked flushed and uncomfortable and I wondered why. My father, however, noticed nothing unusual.

On the *cayo* my stock of tinned food has begun to run out, so this morning I returned with my spear gun to the rampart of the reef. I flattened myself against the floor of the lagoon and peered into the crevice from which I had drawn the lobster in the hope that another might have taken its place there.

I thought at first that the place was deserted; then, from deep within the recess, set in a shapeless mask, all outlines lost in the shadow cast by the overhanging coral, two cold, unblinking eyes stared out at me. My first thought was that a lumbering grouper had taken over the lobster's home. I approached the entrance to the crevice and thrust the muzzle of the spear gun into the shadows.

For a long moment nothing moved; then deep within the crevice there was a violent eruption of sand and water. The aluminium spear gun was almost torn from my grasp. Filling the entrance, swaying like an angry cobra, the orange eyes on fire with threat and malice, I saw the broad head of a moray eel. The cruel jaws opened and closed rhythmically with an air of infinite menace, the long needle teeth very white against the grey interior of the cavernous mouth. The eel's six-foot body, coated with green slime, was coiled like a massive spring within its lair and across the rusty point of my steel arrow I could clearly see the bright traces left by the teeth as they had slipped across the surface of the metal.

I backed slowly away from the wall of the reef, holding the

spear gun at arm's length between me and the grinning face, conscious that at any moment the eel might launch itself at me in a furious burst of energy; conscious, too, that my lungs were crying out for air.

I let my natural buoyancy carry me slowly to the surface, resisting the almost irresistible temptation to kick my way up through the green water. The moray made an evil-tempered lunge at my retreating shadow as it fell across the mouth of the crevice, but it did not follow me up into the open water at the surface.

My head broke through into the sweet, warm air; I spat out the mouthpiece of the snorkel and drew the air into my lungs in shameless, gasping sobs. With my heart hammering against the walls of my chest I retreated across the breadth of the lagoon to search for milder prey in shallower water near the beach.

At the base of a stand of elk-horn coral I saw a fat yellow snapper at rest in the shade. The fish had placed itself between two coral antlers, safe from the attack of any passing barracuda. But it had made no allowance for the slim steel arrow in my gun and I speared it through the gills at my first attempt. The weight of the arrow brought the fish down upon the white sand floor of the lagoon like a shotgun burst brings down a wild duck; it lay there on the sand, the tail jerking feebly, the luminous sulphur colour deserting its flanks with the onset of death.

I fried the fish in coconut oil over the driftwood fire. The pale, fibrous flesh held no flavour but I ate it greedily, hungry for the first time since my arrival. I thought about the great eel lurking out there in its dark cleft in the coral wall, and I wondered idly what might have happened had it followed me to the surface as giant morays are known to do.

The yellow snapper satisfied my hunger. After the meal I pulled on my boots and started off for the fresh-water lake on the far side of the hill to fill my water flasks. The path through the bush which I had last used more than thirty years ago was overgrown but still visible, kept open perhaps by the occasional fisherman who took shelter on the *cayo* in the hurricane season.

I forced my way through a stunted tangle of white cedar and windblown sea grape trees until the ground fell abruptly away beneath my feet and I burst through the undergrowth on to the shore of the lake. Along the margin of the water grew tall ferns and delicate stands of balasier with brilliant, boat-shaped scarlet bracts which hung down to the level of the ground. A few trees swept to the edge of the lake and even advanced some distance into the water. A fine mist hung in their branches and curled in sombre patterns over the surface of the lake. The bright, elliptical mirror of the water reflected a sky pierced with reed stalks.

In the middle of the lake there was a little island, scarcely longer than the fishing canoe which had brought me to the *cayo* and less than half as wide. Like sentries posted to guard the lake and its inhabitants, a pair of white egrets patrolled the shore of the island. Beside them, a trespasser from a less tranquil world, a brown pelican tucked its head beneath its wing and stood dreaming in the afternoon sun.

From the flowers of a purple eupatorium bush on the fringe of the lake a pierid butterfly sailed across the water, borne up by a faint breath of wind which penetrated the screen of trees around it. I watched as the butterfly floated towards the opposite shore. The sunlight trembled on its wings. It sailed on the current of air like some diminutive treasure galleon, an amber jewel set against the blue faience of the lake.

I bought a butterfly once for Simone, all silver filigree and blood-red enamel. We were on holiday in Baranquilla during the second year of our marriage and she had pinned it to her blouse and kissed me hard upon the lips right there in the market place. When we got home she glued it to the mirror of her dressing table and, when I asked her why she did not wear it instead, she replied with that simple sweetness that never failed to charm me: 'If I wear it I might lose it. This way, I shall see it every time I brush my hair and remember that you gave it to me.'

At the edge of the water, not far from where I sat on a fallen tree trunk, there was a flat apron of dried mud raised two feet above the level of the lake. A colony of fiddler crabs had adopted the mud flat as home and I watched as they scavenged for food and kept in order the walls of their tunnels in the mud. When, from time to time, they rested from their work they always took up station at the entrance to their holes with the larger of their two claws barring access to intruders. On the barren surface of the mud they looked like so many pale pink flowers fallen from the branches of the oleander trees above them.

Idly I threw a broken twig on to the mud flat. At once there was a headlong charge towards it and the first crab to arrive snatched up the twig in his outsize claw. When closer examination revealed that the twig was not edible, the fastidious crab carried it off the mud apron and dropped it in the surrounding bush. I threw more twigs; each time there was the same swift rush and the same scramble for possession.

On the slope above the mud flat a ground lizard crossed the rock-strewn earth in pursuit of its unseen prey. A large granite pebble, dislodged by the lizard's careless passage, tumbled down the slope, rolled erratically across the mud and struck one of the crabs squarely on its back. The wounded creature described a little circle on the mud and then fell over on its side, the short legs kicking feebly in the air.

The crab's companions stopped dead in their tracks. Staring with their stalked eyes they closed in to form a circle around their comrade. The stricken crab made a desperate effort to regain its feet, but lurched and fell again on his side. In a split second they were on him, rending, tearing, squabbling among themselves for a position from which to strike.

It was over in less than a minute and the leaders of the mob scuttled away back to their holes with their sinister sideways gait. As they went, I noticed that they carried in their claws, held aloft like trophies of war, the quivering limbs and snow-white flesh of their late companion.

The track that led directly from the lake to the sea skirted a rough platform of earth that appeared once to have been scooped out of the side of the hill. Among the water-worn pebbles and the pallid roots that projected from the bank at the back of the platform there was an object that seemed out of place. It was the size of my fist, lighter in colour than the earth in which it lay and there was something about its symmetry which attracted my attention.

I squatted on the damp earth beneath a twisted guango tree and drew the object from the loose grip of the soil. Its irregular surface was obscured by a cloak of dried mud and I retraced my steps to the lake to wash it clean in the water. From beneath the dissolving mud the image of a human face materialised in my hand, a broad, flat face with bulging eyes, a triangular nose and a deep gash for a mouth. A shaft of sunlight pierced the screen of branches above my head and fell across the inscrutable, unprepossessing features. As surely as if they could speak, they told me something about the *cayo* I had never suspected: there had been people living here long before any member of my own race had set eyes upon it.

At the outer corner of the mouth was the clear impression of a fingerprint, carelessly left by the ancient sculptor while the clay was still wet and fixed forever in the rude kiln which had baked it hard. I placed the tip of my own index finger into the shallow depression; it fitted exactly and I felt an eerie sense of kinship with the dark-skinned man who had fashioned it.

Once, when I was a boy, I had stumbled by chance upon the remains of an Indian settlement along the banks of the stream which flowed past our house on its tortuous journey to the sea. From the wine-dark soil my mother and I had excavated shards of pottery, an undamaged stone axe blade and five of those strangely intimidating clay heads. When our excavation was complete, we used to wander the river

64

bank in the soft light of evening letting our imaginations give human form to the shadows that gathered beneath the tall bamboo where the little Arawak settlement had once stood.

As I squatted at the edge of the lake this afternoon, I thought again about those gentle, inoffensive brown people who had fashioned their curious clay lares wherever they travelled throughout the empty archipelago and then scattered them upon the soil they tilled. What thoughts, I wondered, occupied their minds when they lived on my *cayo* all those years ago? Had they, too, been touched by the beauty of the place or, knowing nothing else, had they taken it all for granted? The man who sculpted the vacant face which lay in my palm, had he loved his broad-hipped woman as I loved mine? Was she faithful to him, or had another man in these enchanted surroundings once suffered the same agony of spirit that my faithless woman had inflicted upon me?

My thoughts turned to Simone. I was unable any longer to suppress the memories which brought the tiger to my throat. For more than five years she had been the rock upon which I had built my life. In the middle of the night, when sleep eluded me, I used to prop myself upon my elbow and watch her in the moonlight which streamed into our room, enchanted by the soft line of her cheek upon the pillow and the play of light and shadow across the swell of her naked breast beside me, scarcely able to believe my good fortune.

The passing of the years only lent strength to my passion. When we made love, I took her with a kind of reverence; it was like entering the propylon of a human temple and when those silken doors closed upon me they shut out the harsh light of the real world for as long as I stayed within her. Afterwards, as I lay silent in her arms, I had to fight anew each time the temptation to tell her how much I loved her.

'He loved me, and he told me so. . .' she said about the man to whom she gave herself. 'I needed to be told. . .'

But I could never do it.

She was only nineteen when I met her, long-legged and skittish as a fawn, with the same swift toss of the head and that characteristic quicksilver flow of movement. She was walking the beach near the holiday cottage I had rented for a week at Negril and her red-gold hair trailed behind her on the morning breeze like the fiery tail of some splendid comet. She was wearing a blue silk halter and a pair of white shorts and her feet were bare.

I had just returned in my dinghy from a dive on the off-shore reef and I was hauling the little craft out of the water with my back towards the trees at the top of the beach. Neither of us was looking where we were going and as I swung the dinghy round on the sand the blunt stern of the plywood vessel brushed against her legs.

She sprang out of the way; I dropped the rope and apologised. She smiled at once to show that I was forgiven and I made some vacuous remark to keep her there with me for a moment. She was used to men who sought to detain her in this way; but she smiled again and looked into the dinghy to admire the silver jack cravalle which lay in the bilge beside my spear gun, still impaled on the steel arrow with which I had shot it half an hour before.

She saw that the arrow had struck the fish behind the eye,

66

the spot for which every experienced fisherman aims.

'You must be clever with that gun,' she said approvingly in her husky voice. 'Jack cravalle move so fast.' She spoke with an accent I could not quite place and she was right about the speed of the elusive jack cravalle.

'I was lucky,' I said. 'This one stopped to say good morning,' and we both laughed at my feeble joke.

I had not shaved that morning because I was alone in the cottage, and I was suddenly conscious of the fact that my swimming trunks were rust stained and torn at the crotch. It was also apparent to me that I was old enough to be her father.

'I'm going to cook the fish for dinner tonight,' I heard myself lie, for I had intended to give it away. 'Would you like to come and help me eat it?'

She hesitated, and I was sure that she was going to refuse. It was not possible that a girl who looked like she did would have no plans for the evening.

'Thank you,' she said at last. 'I can come at seven o'clock, but I won't be able to stay for long.'

I showed her where my cottage stood in the shade of a cluster of almond trees at the top of the sand; she nodded and swung the towel she was carrying over her shoulder and strode on down the beach. The wind caught her hair again and held it out towards me.

'How would you like the fish done?' I called after her.

'Don't fillet it,' she shouted over her shoulder, 'fry it whole.'

I sat down on the gunwale of the dinghy and watched her slim figure recede into the distance until I could no longer make out the blue of her halter against the darker background of the rocks at the end of the long crescent of sand.

I did not really expect to see her again. I began to prepare the fish thinking that I would almost certainly eat it alone. But exactly at seven o'clock I heard her sandalled feet upon the concrete path outside the kitchen and I turned the cravalle in its sea of butter before I went to the door to let her into my house.

She took my hand briefly in hers and then she walked straight into the kitchen.

'Will you let me cook the fish?' she asked; and before I could reply she added: 'I wouldn't want to see it spoiled.'

I was holding the metal spatula in my hand and for a moment I was tempted to bring it down across her trim bottom to reward her for her impudence. But when she looked round at me I saw that her sea-blue eyes were full of laughter. I surrendered the spatula like a defeated general giving up his sword and retreated to the sitting room to pour us each a drink.

When I returned to the kitchen with the drinks in my hand she had put on an apron and turned down the heat under the frying pan. I sat at the small table near the sink intending to watch her at work.

'Oh, no,' she said at once. 'Why don't you have your drink in the other room and I'll bring the fish in as soon as its ready.'

I surrendered again. I sat by myself opposite the door that led to the kitchen, a large whisky in my hand, secretly hoping that she would ruin the fish and so hand me an early tactical advantage. But the cravalle, when she brought it in, was

68

crisp skinned and decorated with green sprigs of parsley, exactly as I liked it. She had found a bottle of white wine in one of the cupboards and she had mixed this in with the melted butter.

When I praised her cooking, she replied simply: 'I wanted to please you.'

Outside, the last trace of the sunset faded and I got up to light the oil lamps. In the pale amber glow that filled the sparsely furnished room I looked at her closely for the first time. Her long red-gold hair cascaded over her bare shoulders and the cornflower eyes returned my gaze without embarrassment.

I noticed that from beneath her right eye to the corner of her mouth there was a hairline scar, visible only because the sun had tanned it just one shade lighter than the velvet skin of her cheek. The scar did not detract from her beauty; in fact it served only to lend to that exquisite face a quality of mystery.

When we had finished the meal she took the dishes out, walked over to the divan and curled up there like a kitten. She was wearing a short white linen skirt which rode up over her thighs; her long legs were tanned dark brown by the sun. She slipped off her sandals and tucked her feet beneath her.

I went out to the kitchen and brought in coffee on a tray; then I uncorked a bottle of brandy and removed two glasses from the cabinet beside the divan. I held up the bottle but she shook her head. I poured a drink for myself and wondered what I could find to talk about that might conceivably be of interest to her. I wanted to know who she was staying with on the beach, but she had not volunteered that information and I could not bring myself to ask. Certainly, I remember thinking, she is far too beautiful to be staying here on her own. Perhaps she had just quarrelled with her lover before I met her and, to teach him a lesson, she had decided to have dinner with another man.

One of my paintings stood on an easel in the corner of the room. It was a watercolour of a Haitian *métisse* on the beach at Cap Haitien; it was evening and the woman was looking out towards a cloud-veiled sun for the sail of her man's canoe. I had sketched the scene from life the day after a hurricane swept across the Windward Passage, and I had tried hard to capture in the woman's dark eyes something of what I had seen there at the time. I had finished the painting only the day before and I had left it on the easel to dry. I was pleased with it.

'Did you paint that?' she inquired.

I nodded.

She sat up and examined the painting in silence.

'Do you like it?' I asked.

'I would prefer to look at it when it's finished,' she said at last.

I was hurt.

'It is finished,' I said sharply.

She laughed that husky, silver laugh that was to delight me so many times in the years which lay ahead.

'I am teasing you,' she said. 'I have seen your work before. It is very good and I admire it.'

There was an ancient gramophone in a scarred wooden cabinet behind the divan; an untidy pile of records lay beside it. I chose the first that came to hand. It was called Strings

70

for Lovers. The pair of gaudy puppets on the jacket had been disfigured by the wet imprint of countless glasses used by previous tenants of the cottage. I held it up for her to see.

'Would you like to hear this?' I asked.

'Yes, please,' she replied. 'That will do very well.'

I switched the gramophone on; there was a series of metallic clicks and groans as the playing arm hoisted itself reluctantly on to the record; then the plain little cottage was filled with silky melody.

I walked over to the drinks cabinet and poured myself another brandy.

'What would you like?' I asked.

She uncurled herself from the divan, cupped my face in her hands and kissed me hard on the lips.

'I would like to make love to you,' she said.

I lifted her up in my arms and carried her back to the divan.

'No,' she said, 'please not here. Take me on your bed.'

Obediently I took her up in my arms again and into the little bedroom. The bed had not been made that morning because I had given my servant the day off. I was conscious of the crumpled sheets hanging limply over the side like the sails of a dismasted schooner.

'Doesn't anyone look after you?' she asked with mock concern.

She stepped out of her clothes. In the light reflected from the oil lamps in the dining room I could just make out the two pale bands that circled her brown body where the silken flesh was covered by her swim suit in the day. Her skin smelt faintly of the sea, the clean, erotic fragrance of the sea.

I kissed her and ran my hands softly over her velvet thighs; at once she opened her legs for me to explore the cleft between them. She turned her face towards me, the mane of golden hair spilling like a waterfall upon my chest.

'Christ,' I whispered, my voice thick with desire for her, 'Christ, you are so beautiful. . .'

I felt her lips move over my body, downwards from my throat. There was a sudden surge of ecstasy like an electric shock. I had not had a woman for more than a month. I turned her gently on her back and took her in my arms.

'I think you are beautiful too,' I heard her say and then we fell together through space and time.

A crescent moon had risen by the time we finished and a single shaft of silver light entered through the open window and fell across her body. She lay there on the bed, breathing lightly, her eyes closed, her hair spread over my pillow in passionate disorder.

She opened her eyes and looked at me without expression in the moonlight. She gave no sign that she was pleased. I had no way of telling whether I had satisfied her. Then she smiled up at me and in that moment, sprawled across the untidy bed fragrant with the scent of our lovemaking, I knew that if I spoke I should be lost. All the resolutions, all the well kept promises I had made to myself so long ago that I would never share my life with any woman, threatened to melt away in her arms.

She took my face in her hands and kissed me.

'I must go now,' she said; and when I laid my hand upon her breast to tempt her to stay a little longer, she removed it.

'I told you at the beginning I couldn't stay for long; but please ask me to come again.'

She slipped out of bed and put her clothes on. I sat naked on a corner of the bed, tongue-tied as a schoolboy. I watched her dress in silence, certain that I was about to lose her forever but determined still that she should not know how I felt about her.

She slipped her feet into her sandals and kissed me chastely on the forehead.

'Will you have dinner with me again tomorrow?' I asked as casually as I could manage.

'I'll come at the same time,' she said at once.

Then she was gone, her light footsteps muffled by the sand at the end of the concrete path. I lay sleepless on the bed, caressing the tangled sheets that still retained the imprint of her naked body.

I have often wondered why she came to love me. Even at that time, while we were getting to know each other on the beach at Negril, I could never understand how it was she seemed to prefer my company to that of the younger men who sought her favour and made no secret of their desire for her.

Her mother was a Frenchwoman from Martinique, related as I afterwards discovered to the family of Tascher de la Pagerie, the creole family of Napoleon's empress, Josephine; her father was a New York banker with a large house on Long Island sound. Her parents had been separated for many years. Since she was seventeen Simone had looked after herself, leaving her querulous, carping mother in Fort-de-France to drift about the West Indian islands, sometimes on her own, more often in the company of some man who had temporarily taken her fancy. Once, when I asked her whether she had been happy with that life, she turned aside my question with a quick shake of the head and the comment that she had learnt never to look backwards.

I was nearly twice her age when we met, my hair already greying at the temples, and it was quite clear by that time that my pictures were never going to make me a wealthy man. Simone loved the excitement of travel, the constant change of scene, the predictable unpredictability of moving from one place to another; and she knew that except for my regular visits to Haiti my work chained me to my easel at home for eleven months of the year. Yet, in spite of this, when my extended holiday at Negril finally drew to an end and I asked her to marry me, she replied at once with no trace of hesitation: 'Oh, yes please. I would like to do that more than anything in the world.'

I remember how my heart leapt with an inexpressible joy, and how I forced myself to say simply: 'Good. Well that's settled then. . .'

And that night, when I was alone, I remember how I said to myself, to reassure that part of me which doubted the wisdom of what I had done: You can have her for your wife without chaining yourself to her; you can have her and keep your distance at the same time. There is no need for you to get hurt, no matter what may happen.

There have been times since then in our lives together when I used to think that if I could I would have enclosed her in a case of glass, like a butterfly in its cabinet, where I could delight in the look of her whenever I chose and from which comfortable confinement no one else could ever entice her. I never tried to paint her portrait, knowing that my hand could not do justice to the perfect oval of her face or to the colour of her hair and, over the years, I have taken less than a dozen casual photographs of her. So now I shall have little more than my memory to fall back on when I wish to look at her again.

After we were married Simone at once took charge of my home and guarded me fiercely from the unwelcome attentions of people who sought to interrupt me while I painted. She did her best to like my friends, all of them so much older than herself. In time the difference in our ages began to seem to me of no account and in our third year together I came at last to believe her when she said she loved me. I think this joy was reflected in the quality of my paintings where the drab greens and greys I once preferred were replaced by emphatic blues and purples and that lustrous golden red that was the colour of her hair.

I walked down to the beach this evening to watch the pageant of the sunset. The clouds above the western horizon had taken the shape of knights on horseback and their purple pennants streamed across the darkening sky, drawn out and then cut loose by the tide of the wind. To keep my mind from any further thought of Simone I tried to recall memories of my early childhood, but for some reason the bright images I sought to conjure up remained stubbornly out of reach. I could think only of my mother, and my thoughts of her were bitter as gall.

My mother left me when I was thirteen. She ran away with Marcus, that gentle, unassuming man who had come every year with us to our cottage in the mountains. The blow fell upon me without warning. One moment she was there and life proceeded on its pleasant course; the next, she had packed her clothes, all those elegant, expensive evening dresses among them, and she was gone. I was left behind to listen to my father attempting in his stiff, impassive way to explain to me that my mother preferred to spend the rest of her life with another man. And she had left me no message, not even kissed me goodbye.

For the next two days I remained in my room, feigning sleep whenever I heard the approaching footsteps of someone who wished to comfort me. I did not see my father. Later, I learnt that he had spent most of those first desolate days in the saddle of his horse galloping aimlessly around the wide perimeter of his land, for like me he had loved her with a passionate devotion. His labourers, who knew what had happened, took shelter within the tall sugar cane as he passed by in his agony, so to him the fields must have appeared deserted; but he never noticed.

For myself, I prayed without hope that death would claim me.

It was, I think, about ten days after my mother's departure that I first overheard the house servants discussing the drama. They had gathered in a little knot at the foot of the steps which led from the landing outside my room to the downstairs pantry. They were worried about the future, both for me and for themselves, for they all had children of their own. Their hushed, sepulchral voices drifted up the narrow stairway and through the open door beyond my bed.

'Now who could have believed she would just go off so, widout even tellin' de young Massa goodbye,' I heard old Ethel the cook say. 'An' all de time she mek out she love him so much.'

'How could she ever do a t'ing like dat?' one of the others asked. And then, more anxiously: 'You t'ink she ever goin' come back?'

'Well, you can see dat she never really love de boy at all,' Ethel replied. 'She was jus' play actin' all de time. All she really love was dressin' up and showin' off sheself at all dem parties. . .'

'I wonder if de young Massa ever goin' excuse her?'

'If it was me,' Ethel said sharply, 'I could never forgive such a t'ing. But mebbe, after all, she goin' come back.'

There was a long pause; then Christiana, my Haitian nurse, spoke for the first time: 'You all listen to me,' she said, her rich voice full of quiet authority. 'We jus' have to come togedder an' mek sure de young Massa don' feel no one care 'bout him. When de time ripe, I goin' tek him up de mountain to see de *houngan*. Mebbe de *houngan* can cause de Mistress to come back; an' if not, den it is somet'ing de boy have a right to know.'

There was a murmur of general approval.

'An' de rest of us too,' I heard Ethel say.

'Yes,' agreed Christiana. 'All of us have a right to know what goin' happen.'

The voices died away as the servants returned to the kitchen. I lay on my bed to think about Christiana's intention to take me to the mountain and to search my memory for some previous mention of the *houngan*. But I could not recall having heard that name before.

More than three months were to pass by after that overheard conversation before I learnt what Christiana meant. My father had driven across the mountains to Kingston to instruct his lawyers about the divorce he was now determined to have. He had arranged to spend the night in the capital and I was left in the custody of Christiana and the other servants.

When Christiana came to my room in the middle of the afternoon, I think that I was half expecting her.

'Massa Michael,' she said without preamble, 'I want to tek you to see someone who can tell you 'bout you mother.'

'What can they tell me that I don't know already?' I asked.

'Dey can tell you wedder she ever goin' come back.'

I said nothing.

'You will come wid me, young Massa?' she asked anxiously.

'Where?' I wanted to know, although I was already in possession of that information.

'Up de mountain. If de two of us leave now we can reach back here before de night too old.'

'All right,' I said. 'But if this person can really see the future I want you to ask about me too. I want to know about my own life.'

'I will ask,' she replied, and she left to find my boots and to make herself ready for the journey.

We followed the steep, rocky track which coiled its way

up from the flat fields of cane into the heart of the mountains. The air became perceptibly cooler as we left the plain below us. Giant guango trees, their branches festooned with bearded epiphytes, towered over the path. In the dense forest on either side of the track only an occasional shaft of slanted sunlight pierced the gloom beneath the canopy of leaves. Clouds gathered above the trees and soon it began to rain; the run-off from the slopes higher up the mountain raced across the track in musical streams of cold, crystal water. It was at once both fearful and enchanting.

Christiana and I climbed in silence, saving our breath for the steepest sections of the track where it was necessary to haul ourselves up by the exposed tree roots which every-where burst through the rich, rain-eroded soil.

As darkness was falling over the plain below us we arrived at a clearing in the forest beneath an ancient silk cotton tree. At one side of the clearing there was a simple mud and wattle hut; at the other side stood the *tonnelle*, a long, palm-thatched structure open at the front. I noticed that the hard-packed mud floor was chequered with rust-coloured stains. The unmistakable stench of dried blood hung heavily about the place.

In the deep gloom at the far end of the *tonnelle* a very old woman was crouched on a wooden stool, evidently waiting for us to approach. She was a frail, bird-like creature and her coal-black face was wrinkled and furrowed like the outer husk of a fallen coconut. Only her eyes were young, and they seemed to burn in that ancient face with a curious incandes-cence.

The woman was wearing a stained white robe which

79

trailed on the ground and there was a turban of the same material wrapped tightly around her skull. In the darkness behind her, at the back of the *tonnelle*, I could just make out a cluster of wooden cages and black, coffin-shaped receptacles with ill-formed hieroglyphics scrawled in white paint along their sides. In front of them stood a low wooden cross and draped over it was a morning coat surmounted by a black top hat.

Christiana tugged me firmly by the hand and together we approached the silent old woman.

'*C'est moi, Maman, c'est Christiana,*' she said softly. 'I have brought the white boy with me.'

The old woman grunted and rose painfully from her stool.

'Come into the hut with me, Christiana,' she said in the guttural French patois of her native Haiti. 'Leave M'sieur the white boy here for a while.'

I squatted uncomfortably on the hard mud floor and waited. In the thick bush which surrounded the *tonnelle* the creatures of the night began their whistling, chuckling chorus. I shivered a little in the chill mountain air.

It was quite dark when the old woman returned to the *tonnelle* with Christiana, a guttering tallow candle in her hand. She motioned me to sit beside Christiana on the floor. From a chest at the back of the *tonnelle* she fetched a curved French cavalry sword with a tarnished silver hilt, and with the point of the weapon she described two perfect circles in the dust beside me. Then from one of the cages I had seen earlier, masked now by the darkness behind her, she withdrew two fowls, a black cockerel and a white hen. She trussed their legs and tossed the hen into the circle beside Christiana and the cockerel into the one nearest me. Using the point of the sword as a trowel, she excavated a shallow channel in the mud floor connecting one circle with the other.

The old woman put down the sword and took up a tall drum from the shadows. She began to beat an erratic rhythm upon it and circled the floor of the *tonnelle* in time with the beat of the drum. In a thin, cracked voice she started to sing: '*Venez mon Dieu*,' she chanted, '*venez mon doux Sauveur, venez mon Dieu. . .*'

She turned faster and faster across the floor. Imperceptibly, her invocation to the Saviour became a plea to the ancient Gods of West Africa.

'*Venez Mama Lwa*,' she shouted, '*venez Papa Legba, venez Ogoun Ferraile. . .*'

One by one the Gods of voodoo were summoned from their homes across the ocean to that lonely *tonnelle* in the mountains of Jamaica. As each dark divinity arrived among us and took possession of her body, the old woman emitted a piercing shriek of ecstasy.

The drum beat faster and faster, the old woman whirled her withered body in tighter and tighter circles; with a final climactic shriek of triumph she fell to the floor beside the two circles she had drawn in the dust.

There was a long moment of silence in the *tonnelle*, broken only by the old woman's rasping intake of breath. Then she picked herself up, squatted on her haunches and addressed Christiana: 'Tell this white boy you have brought here,' she said in patois, 'tell him that we shall see now if I can join his mother and his father once again.'

The flame of the tallow candle was drawn out by a gust of

wind. The shadows danced dementedly across the thatched ceiling. The old woman's formidable personality seemed to expand to fill the stark building; I had no doubt at that moment that she could indeed see into the uncharted future.

I found it difficult to breathe; a great weight hung about my shoulders forcing the breath from my lungs. I wanted to stand up, to run out of the oppressive hut into the cool night air; but my legs had lost their strength. I looked sideways at Christiana. Her eyes were tightly closed and I could see that she had entered a state of trance.

The old woman began a sacred incantation: '*Lade im-memeenou dauginin soilade anguignaminsou . . . pingolo, pingolo roi monter nous la prie qui minin africain* . . . Oh, Oh, Oh. . .'

The incantation seemed to last forever; then it was over. There was a moment of complete silence. With a shriek which brought Christiana out of her trance the old woman flung herself from the place where she was squatting and grabbed the fowls by their necks. There were two distinct cracks as the vertebrae snapped beneath her bony fingers. From somewhere within her robe she drew a knife and with two swift strokes she decapitated the fowls. The headless bodies twitched and jerked frantically within the circles drawn for them in the dust. The blood spouted from their necks and ran across the circles; but it stopped short of the little drains she had excavated in the mud floor. The twin pools of blood swelled but did not join each other; each stayed glistening in the candlelight within its own set boundary.

I looked up at the old woman's face. In the pale light of the guttering candle it was bathed in sweat and her eyes were as red as the blood of the fowls. With the point of the sword she disembowelled one of the twitching corpses and spread the entrails over the floor. She gazed intently at the stinking mess, reading what it had to say about me and my future. Addressing Christiana again she clasped her reeking hands about my throat and spoke in a voice so faint that I could scarcely hear her, the mumbled patois words tumbling in a whispered monotone from her lips.

Then she collapsed on the floor of the *tonnelle*, frail and dry as an autumn leaf in her exhaustion, and almost instantly she was asleep.

Christiana and I returned in silence down the steep mountain path, helped on our way by an early rising three-quarter moon. We arrived home drained and footsore. I waited until we had climbed the last step to the front verandah.

'Well, what did she say?' I demanded.

Christiana wrapped her arms about me and hugged me to her bosom.

'De *houngan* say it is no good,' she said sadly. 'De blood would not flow togedder. Mistress never goin' come back. She goin' sen' for you instead.'

In the pale light a pair of cave bats wheeled above the garden, their fragile wings silhouetted against the face of the three-quarter moon.

'And what did she see about me in the guts of the chicken?' I asked. 'What did she tell you when she had her stinking hands around my throat?'

Christiana hesitated.

'Well go on,' I prompted. 'You promised me.'

'De *houngan* say you will grow up to be a prideful man,' she replied at last.

'Is that all?'

'No, young Massa. She say dat out of all dis trouble good can come to you.'

'How?' I asked.

'She say dat dis trouble mus' teach you to be hard as iron. She say dat if you never trus' anodder woman, if you never forget nor forgive, den nothin' can hurt you again. She say dat if you learn de lesson from all dis, den dat will be your armour an' your protection.'

'What did she mean by that?' I asked.

'I don' know exactly, young Massa,' Christiana replied. 'Maybe de ol' woman herself didn' properly understan'. It was just what she read in de chicken guts.'

That night in bed, before exhaustion closed my eyes, I repeated to myself that conversation word for word. 'I am going to be hard as iron,' I whispered to myself in the darkness. 'From now on I shall trust no one. I shall not be hurt again.' And the thought pleased me; but almost immediately, rearing up behind it, I could perceive the awkward shadow of a conflict.

For as far back as I could remember, I had taken it for granted that overseeing my presence on earth was a compassionate God; and such a God, I knew, would never approve the *houngan*'s counsel. Until that moment I had never really questioned that God existed. I had after all only to look at the pattern of colour on a butterfly's wing or examine the immaculate spiral of an auger shell to see all the proof of his existence that I needed.

That belief had survived my mother's desertion, for I could not see that anyone else might be held responsible for her treachery, but now it was challenged by the old woman's words. The more I thought about it, the more I was determined to take that counsel; only if I became hard and unforgiving would I armour myself against all future hurt; but how could I reconcile this with a God who promised – and required – the gentle quality of forgiveness?

And so the conflict was born in my mind and, from time to time in the months that followed, it drove me out of the house to wander the banks of the stream at the end of our garden, searching unhappily for the answers that I needed, oblivious to the antics of the crayfish on the gravel bottom and to the hollow voice of the bamboo groves.

It was not long after my visit to the *houngan* that my father received a letter from my mother. I remember as if it were yesterday how he came to my room that evening. He was carrying the letter in his hand and he held it at arm's length as if it had been contaminated with the ashes of hell.

'Your mother wants you to go to live with her,' he said without preamble, in a voice as dry and dead as an echo in the bowl of a rotten tree. 'She thinks you would be better off there.'

Across the stream at the bottom of the garden I could hear the subdued chatter of the labourers making their way back to their families after the long day's work in the fields. It was drizzling fitfully outside and to protect his hair from the rain each man held a banana leaf above his head, the loose sides of the leaf falling like a curtain below the level of his ears. From the window of my room I could see the green testudo snaking along the slippery path in the direction of the barracks.

So the *houngan* was right, I thought. She had sent for me.

'Do you want to go?' my father asked at last. 'It is for you to decide.'

If you never forget nor forgive, the *houngan* had declared, nothing can hurt you again.

'No,' I said, my heart bursting with love for my mother and hurt for what she had done to me.

'Very well,' he said quietly; and in what for him was the rarest of gestures, he laid the open palms of his hands against my cheeks before he left the room.

He never told me what reply he sent to my mother's letter, but she did not ask me to come to her again.

On the spur of a hill near the boundary of our estate, almost lost in a field of cane which surged right up to the broken walls, stood the remains of a sugar factory. A giant banyan tree sprang from the centre of the ruins and the wide network of roots bound together the crumbling blocks of limestone and helped delay the complete collapse of the old building. Only the tall chimney still rose intact from the wreckage, a thin, gaunt finger pointing without purpose to the sky.

I often rode my donkey down to the ruined factory to scramble over the decaying walls and to picture it in my imagination as it must have looked at the beginning of the last century. The old cane press with its clumsy hardwood rollers and iron cog wheels had long since disappeared, but half buried in the debris of the boiling house I once found a huge iron cauldron. A thin crack ran unevenly from the flared lip of the cauldron towards its centre and I suppose, because of this flaw, no one had ever thought it worth removing.

On the tallest remaining section of the factory wall was a pair of rusting iron rings. They were embedded firmly in the masonry and hung about seven feet above the ground, and it was from them that delinquent slaves were once strung up to be flogged until they slumped unconscious against the bloodstained wall.

It was in this sad place that I sought refuge that evening, and it was there, beneath the iron rings, that I swore to myself a solemn oath: for the rest of my life, however long or short, I would resist with all my strength the temptation to love or trust another woman.

In the years to come, obedient to my oath, I sought pleasure and satisfaction in the sight and use of their bodies but, until the day I met Simone, I was always able to discard them afterwards like so much spoiled fruit.

Friday, June 23rd

I slept badly last night. I dreamed that I had returned to Simone, that somehow I had managed to curb my pride.

'I forgive you,' I said; and though I had to tear the words from my throat, I spoke them.

In my dream we had just made love and I had already entered that familiar, rapturous state when I used to hold her in my arms, my physical desire vanquished by a deeper, more tender emotion. She slept with her head in the crook of my arm, the towel still between her legs, the velvet warmth of her body pressed against the rougher contours of my own. I experienced once again that curious sense of triumph that fills a man when he has satisfied his woman and heard beneath him her primeval cry of ecstasy.

But in my dream Simone did not remain beside me. Though my eyes were closed I saw her slip silently out of bed, bending low over my body to make sure that I was asleep. I watched her run to the window of our room. There was another man standing there. He was fully dressed and she came to him as she was, naked except for the towel still held between her legs. She reached up to him and kissed him on the mouth and the towel fell to the floor between them. The man's face was hidden in shadow but I could see his body clearly in the moonlight and he took her there against the window frame. I watched her face light up with a pulsating inner radiance and upon it I could see the same ecstatic expression which I had witnessed only a few minutes earlier when she had given herself to me.

I watched their bodies moving together at the window. They clung to each other with increasing urgency until there was a sudden climactic burst of light. I saw her cry out in joy, a wild, passionate cry I had never heard before; then I woke up in my cramped shelter on the *cayo* my body bathed in sweat, my heart hammering against the walls of my chest, my spirit rebelling in agonised protest against what I had just witnessed in my dream.

I crawled out of the shelter and walked unsteadily down the sand to the edge of the sea. On impulse, I threw myself full length into the cool water. The sharp shock hauled me out of the tunnel of my dream. The sun had not yet risen, but above the eastern horizon a strip of cloud was already lit by a fire of green and gold. On the slope of the hill behind me the waxy sea grape leaves glittered with dew. High over the lagoon a pair of scissor-tailed frigate birds wheeled together in lazy circles across the empty sky. Beyond the crescent reef the rising breeze whipped off the unsteady crown of each passing wave and spread an ephemeral pattern of white foam across the blue water.

The sun rose as I waded out of the sea, the sudden flood of warmth falling about my naked body like a blanket. The bitter memory of the dream began to lose its hold upon me; I squatted on the tall bank of sand raised by last night's high water and looked around me at the waking island. The air was fragrant with the scent of giant morning glory which climbed in tangled profusion over the fallen trunk of a nearby coconut palm.

'The *houngan* was right,' I whispered to myself, eager to repudiate my conduct in the dream. 'I am a hard man; I will not forgive people who wound me.'

A gust of wind caught my words and carried them away to the sea. I returned to my shelter, lit the driftwood fire in the hearth and hung the metal coffee pot above the flames.

In the same pitted limestone platform where I had found the fallow deer cowry when I was a boy, the retreating tide leaves behind it twice each day a deeper pocket of water. For two or three hours in every twenty-four this submarine world has an independent existence of its own. When I passed the place this morning the on-shore breeze had died away and the polished surface of the pool reflected my drawn, unsmiling face as faithfully as any silvered mirror.

Beneath the cap of glass the colours had an electric brilliance. There were reds and mauves and every conceivable shade of green and blue; and yet I noticed that the colours never seemed to clash as they would if I were to use them together on a canvas. There was a natural harmony and balance in that small circle of water, with its ribbons of milky light reaching down to the carpet of white sand.

This morning, all around the jagged rim of the pool sheets of translucent sea lettuce floated upon the surface of the water, spread out in the sunlight like a mermaid's chartreuse hair. An antler of stag-horn coral, torn from the reef by some forgotten storm, lay half buried in the sand, a solitary coral tine pointing up towards my mirrored face.

In the very centre of the pool there was a living stand of fire coral, the delicate, fluted blades rising from the uneven floor like the pipes of some sea-distorted organ. Jewel-studded damselfish flirted among the organ pipes, indifferent to my long shadow which fell across them.

The tide was running out and I saw that the retreating sea had trapped together in the pool two fish from the open sea which had lingered too long in the shallows. One of the fish was a female mullet; the other a young barracuda. I watched as the diminishing area of the pool inexorably drew them closer to each other. Little tumbling overspills at the edge of the pool took more and more water away to the retreating sea until the depth of the depression in the middle of the pool was less than my own height. At that moment the mullet saw the barracuda for the first time.

The panic-stricken fish raced blindly about the pool, colliding with every sharp underwater projection, shedding silver scales in its wake. The barracuda retreated to one corner of the pool and waited; only those cold, cunning eyes moved as it followed every twist and turn of the mullet's erratic course. As the minutes passed the mullet's mad progress became perceptibly slower; the barracuda, I noticed, had not moved at all.

Without warning, the mullet's energy gave out. The plump silver fish rose to the surface, the forked tail beating feebly, the gills straining for oxygen. On its flanks there were raw, pink patches where the scales had been struck off against the limestone. At that moment the patient barracuda drove out of its corner, struck the mullet behind the pectoral fins and tore it neatly in half. I stood at the edge of the pool and watched the two quivering halves of the mullet slide down through the green water. They came to rest side by side on the white sand. The severed tail raised a little cloud of debris around it and then was still.

I was not moved by the incident. That the exquisite microworld of the pool should merely be another setting for cruel death did not seem unjust to me this morning. The fat mullet had made an error of judgement by remaining a minute too long in the pool when the rest of its school had left on the ebbing tide. Blind chance had caused the barracuda to commit the same error on the same tide. The lesson was clear: every creature must bear the consequences of its own behaviour. It applied to the mullet, and it applied equally to my wife. There was no forgiveness in the rock pool.

At noon today the sky became overcast and a light rain began to fall. A wall of cloud moved in from the east, hiding the sun and bringing with it a thicker curtain of rain which lashed the sea around the island. The wind rose to a light gale and I noticed that beyond the reef which protected the lagoon there was a big sea running.

The tide came in at about two o'clock and soon, in quick succession, long, dark waves with boiling crests began to break over the rampart of the reef. An uneasy twilight fell like a blanket over the *cayo*; the darkened distance glittered with lightning shafts. The wind howled off the water and the coconut palms all around me bent low before the violence of the storm, their feathered boughs folded back over their crowns like bottle-green umbrellas blown inside out. Some of the weaker boughs were torn loose and one crashed down on the sand at the entrance to my shelter where I had unwisely chosen to sit out the storm.

The rain beat with increasing fury on the thatched roof and the frail structure trembled wildly to the erratic rhythm of the wind. I crawled outside to see if I could secure the roof more firmly to its bamboo supports, but in that maelstrom of flying sand and water there was nothing I could do. I retreated into the shelter wet and cold, unaware that what I had experienced up to then was only a precursor of the real storm which was bearing down upon the island.

When it arrived a little after four o'clock it overwhelmed the *cayo* with a terrible ferocity. There seemed no longer to be any distinction between air and water. Out on the reef the howling wind ripped the tops off the mountainous waves and flung them in solid sheets of spray against the fabric of the island. It was no longer possible to look into the face of the storm. The unleashed sea surged high over the reef and fell against the open, unprotected beach; it raced over the level plain on which I had raised my shelter, foaming about the naked trunks of the coconut palms, clutching at everything in its broad path.

I felt the little shelter quiver ominously; then the thatched roof was torn from its supports and sailed into the air like a giant kite. A cataract of water fell in upon me. The wind screamed across the plain tearing at my hair, driving sand into my eyes and nostrils.

I crawled out of the shell of my hut, grabbed the canvas bag that held my clothes and fled blindly through the curtain of water towards the face of the granite cliff. Beneath a ledge of rock there was a narrow cave which I remembered from one of my previous visits. On that occasion I had dug up the floor of the cave in the hope that some unknown buccaneer might once have thought it a good place to bury his treasure; but I had uncovered only sharp-edged flakes of rock and the calcified skeleton of an ancient sea bird. Now I crept into this refuge like a hunted animal. I lay down on the cratered hard mud floor, my body shaking with cold. Searching fingers of icy water had already found their way into the cave through a fissure in the ceiling and a party of ground lizards, their natural fear overcome by the threat of the storm, crept past me to take shelter in the dark at the far end of the cave.

The storm blew itself out late in the afternoon and almost immediately the thick wall of cloud which had concealed the sun passed across the sky and melted away over the southern horizon. The sun reappeared in a sky washed clean by the rain; the injured *cayo* steamed in the heat. At the back of the cave the quiescent ground lizards stirred uneasily and, gathering their courage, made a sudden dash for the opening. I felt their smooth, waxy bodies brush against my bare forearm; then they were gone, racing back to their own shelters among the fallen rocks at the base of the cliff.

I hauled myself out of the cave and walked across the steaming plain of sand back to the remains of my shelter. The bamboo supports leant drunkenly against each other and the thatched side walls lay flat on the wet sand; but the contents of the shelter and the few remaining tins of food were still there.

I hung out my clothes and bedding to dry in the sun and set to work to repair the damage in the hour of daylight which still remained. By late evening, with the purple shadows gathering beneath the sea grape trees, the work was done. I sat on the damp sand above the high-water mark and watched the tail of the storm rage on across the sea towards the distant mainland of Jamaica. The steel-grey water still thundered against the coral rampart of the reef and the gentle contours of the beach had been replaced by sharp-edged banks of sand; tall, unsightly drifts stood beside deep scars in the surface of the beach from which they had been gouged by the waves. But already the pale ghost crabs, which had survived the storm deep within their holes, were driving fresh tunnels through the sand, and I knew that by the time I was ready to leave the drifts would have been laid flat again and no lasting trace of the storm's assault would be visible on the golden beach.

Two hundred and fifty years ago, the first member of my family to settle in the West Indies was saved by a storm like the one I have just witnessed. He had sailed with his wife and son from Plymouth to Jamaica to take advantage of the Government's offer of free grants of land to Englishmen who wished to be their own masters. With six gold sovereigns in a money belt strapped around his waist, James Hobart had taken passage for the Caribbean in a leaky, ill-found merchantman.

When the family arrived in Jamaica, however, they found that the plot of land they had been allocated along the south coast was too riddled with salt to produce any worthwhile crops, and they lacked the money to drain the soil and wash the salt away. It soon dawned upon them that far from creating a better life for themselves in the Caribbean, they would have to work harder than the black slaves on the plantations around them simply to remain alive. Life, which had appeared so full of new promise, degenerated into a harsh, remorseless struggle to survive.

The money with which they had arrived in Jamaica dwindled until there remained only a handful of copper coins, and there was nothing to show for it but an acre of straggling, thin-stemmed sugar cane whose value would not even meet the cost of hiring a cart to take it to the nearest factory.

The great hurricane of 1777 struck the south coast of Jamaica at night. Jonas and his family had time only to take cover in a little circle of boulders on a pinnacle of land that overlooked their frail mud and wattle hut. From that place of shelter they saw, when a watery daylight replaced the shrieking pitch-black night, that their house had gone. A torrent of brown water raced over the site, sweeping away the mound on which the hut had stood, re-shaping the contours of the land over which it passed. They had owned little; the hurricane left them with nothing but their lives and the rags in which they were dressed.

As the angry water receded from the land, Timon, their son, left his parents huddled in the sparse shelter of the boulders and wandered aimlessly towards the beach across what had been their field of cane.

Where there was once a low rampart of sand raised above the level of the surrounding land, there was now a shallow depression. As Timon looked with tired, indifferent eyes at the transformation which had taken place, something on the sand less than a yard from where he stood caught the light of the sun. He knelt and saw that it was an ill-shaped silver coin, not worn with use but as clean and fresh as the day it had come from the mint. Beyond it there was another and then another, the path of silver leading towards a hole in the sand from which the sunlight was reflected from a thousand separate coins.

Timon had thrust his hand deep into the hole and for as far down as he could reach he felt only the cold, smooth touch of the coins. He tore off his ragged, sweat-stained shirt and filled it with the coins. Then he raced back across the steaming earth to the shelter among the boulders and without a word he poured the contents of his shirt on to the wet mud floor until the coins spilled over the feet of his parents in a river of shining silver.

Those glistening pieces of eight, an Officer's share perhaps of Henry Morgan's Panama treasure, brought ditches to our waterlogged land and, in good time, a full measure of prosperity to our family in the West Indies. It was one story my father never tired of telling and, as he always told it in the same sonorous phrases, eventually I came to know them by heart.

This evening, however, as I stood on the sand contemplating the storm-damaged beach I wondered for the first time whether it might not have been better for me had my ancestor Timon never found those bright silver coins to which I owe my own existence.

I sat out on the sand at the top of the beach tonight. There was no moon; the stars trembled in their appointed places. I looked up at the sky and recalled I had read that there were as many stars in that infinity as there are grains of sand upon all the beaches of the world.

I took up a handful of loose sand, still warm from the afternoon sun that had followed the storm, and let the coral grains slide through my open fingers. I tried to imagine how many grains there might be in that one handful, and how many handfuls composed the beach in front of me, and how many beaches there were all over the world; and not for the first time I considered the possibility that our universe might be no more than a grain of sand on the beach of yet another universe, and so on through an infinite number of universes without end. But though all this reminded me of the true scale of my own importance in the scheme of things, it gave me no comfort.

This sombre train of thought brought back to me the precise moment when, nearly a year after my visit to the *houngan*, my belief in God finally snapped like a sun-dried reed and so at last resolved the conflict between that belief and the *houngan*'s cold advice.

I was at dinner with my father when Christiana's granddaughter pulled over on to herself a kerosene tin of water which had been left boiling for my bath on the wood stove in our kitchen.

For more than eight hours the little girl's cries of agony echoed through the house until she died at last as the sun was rising next morning. All down her chest to the fork of her legs the black skin hung in shrivelled folds and her shrieks did not abate until, far too late, with a dispassionate, indifferent mercy, death cut short her final tormented scream.

I knew the little girl well; in the dusty yard outside the

kitchen I often picked her up and swung her on to my shoulders.

'Go, massa race horse,' she used to yell in my ear, digging her bare heels hard into my ribs, 'gallop like hell.'

Her grandmother's scandalised face would appear in the kitchen window. 'Don' you talk to de young Massa like dat,' Christiana would shout; but horse and rider would be far away by that time, scattering behind them a trail of dust and laughter.

Just before she died, the little girl looked up at me and begged in her extremity: 'Lift me up, massa race horse, lift me up one more time.' But we had already galloped our last gallop.

Afterwards, I sat with my father on the verandah of our house, watching the sun rise over the jewelled fields of sugar cane as if nothing in the world had changed during the course of the night.

'Why?' I demanded to know. 'Why didn't God prevent it?'

My father was silent. I pressed him for an answer.

'I'm afraid it is the old conundrum,' he said at last. 'If there is a God, then it stands to reason that either he must be all-powerful or he must be all-good. He can hardly be both, or such things as happened last night would not be possible; so we must take our choice.'

I saw at once the force of the argument. The only God in whom I could believe had to be both these things. As the sun lifted the dew from the blades of sugar cane so my belief evaporated. I was suddenly free of the conflict which had racked me since the night of my visit to the *houngan*.

A chill wind swept down from the slope of the hill behind me, its light fingers playing in the branches of the coconut palms above my head. I was overwhelmed by an ineffable sadness, an intolerable longing for the warmth of a comfort which I could not explain even to myself. I was racked by a sense of desolation, of incompleteness, of separation from something infinitely desirable but always beyond my furthest grasp.

I struggled to give shape in my mind to what it was I wanted, but perversely it seemed to grow increasingly formless and out of focus the closer I approached it. I knew for certain only that it had to do with love, love given and love received.

Squatting there on the sand in the blue-black darkness of the night, I was suddenly reminded of that haunting definition of Hell: it is a place where a man is excluded from the light of God's presence. You discover for certain that, after all, there is a God; but you find that he has turned his back upon you forever, and the knowledge burns deeper than the cruellest flame.

But, of course, I believed in no God.

I crept unhappily into my shelter with its freshly thatched roof and I pulled the sleeping bag tight about my shoulders. But the conviction persisted that somewhere out there, beyond the most distant star perhaps, there was a state of love and enduring beauty and a spectrum of bright colours without a beginning or an end, and an all-pervading compassion and understanding; a refuge where human pride was as out of place as the Devil himself. But if I had ever known the secret of how to find the road to that place, I knew that I had lost it long ago.

The sense of desolation remained with me in the shelter. Once again the longing for my wife threatened to unleash the tiger at my throat.

'God help me,' I pleaded, in spite of my unbelief.

Saturday, June 24th

When I woke this morning the surf was no longer thundering against the reef. The voice of the island was once again the passage of the wind through the palm fronds and the shrill counterpoint of the laughing gulls wheeling and diving over the windward shore.

It was my forty-fifth birthday. I lay cocooned in my sleeping bag and forced my brain to work out how many days those years embraced. Because I was still half asleep I kept losing track of the multiplication. Eventually I arrived at a figure of 16,425. I did the sum again and with much satisfaction I got the same result. Then I remembered that I had made no allowance for leap years and, because I could not recall in what year the last of these had fallen, I gave up.

What have I accomplished in all those thousands of mornings and afternoons that together made up the pastiche of my life? What would a balance sheet show?

Seven – perhaps ten – pictures that I am not at all ashamed of, and three of these on permanent exhibition in galleries that I admire. A few close-set paragraphs in glossy guides to contemporary art and artists: 'A lyric painter with his own uncompromising view of the world about him. . . An artist engaged in an endless love affair with the colours on his palette . . . a man who may yet fulfil the bright promise of his early work. . .'

It is not much to show for forty-five years of life, and nothing at all to set against the failure of a marriage.

On the beach the debris thrown up by the storm crackled beneath my feet; the ghost crabs which had been feeding on it retreated to their holes at my approach, or sought temporary refuge in the steel-grey water. I looked out across the lagoon, shading my eyes against the diamond light.

The tide was running out and on the reef the tops of the lattice-work sea fans were already exposed to the morning sun. Many of the larger sea fans had been carried away by yesterday's surf and their shredded skeletons lay bleaching on the sand. On one side of the narrow passage through the coral I saw what at first careless glance I thought was the storm-tossed trunk of a coconut palm. There was something about its shape, however, about the regular curve of either end, which caused me to look more closely. At once I saw that the 'tree trunk' was in fact a boat, smaller but not unlike the fishing canoe which had brought me to the *cayo*. The stump of its bamboo mast projected above the level of the gunwale and there were deep gouges in the green paint along the side where it had been flung against the reef. I climbed on to the coral obelisk at the top of the beach to get a better view: inside the stranded vessel, one arm hanging limply over the side, the fingers trailing in the water, there was the body of a man.

I cupped both hands to my mouth and shouted across the water. I thought I saw the arm move in response, but I could not be sure. I waded into the lagoon and started to swim towards the reef, helped on my way by the ebbing tide.

Half-way across I trod water and shouted again; this time

the man in the canoe raised his head for a brief moment above the level of the gunwale. I saw the mouth open in an effort to reply to my call, but no sound came from him and the head fell back to the bottom of the canoe as if the effort had been too great to sustain.

I reached the edge of the coral and hauled myself out of the water and on to the firm carcase of the reef. The canoe was held lightly at the bows; as far as I could see, the thick hull was undamaged and the tide had not yet ebbed far enough to wedge it firmly between the coral heads on which it rested. I moved cautiously along the exposed surface of the reef among the injured sea fans, avoiding the long-spined black sea urchins which had survived the storm and still infested every crevice in the face of the coral.

The man was lying on his back in the bottom of the canoe, his bare legs in the water which had run to the stern of the vessel as the retreating tide had served to raise the bows. Had he been facing the other way, he would have drowned inside his own canoe.

He was an old black man clad only in a pair of ragged khaki shorts and his breathing was heavy and irregular. I put my hands beneath his arms and hauled him to a sitting position with his back against the bow locker, his feet resting on the seat through which the stump of the bamboo mast projected. He opened his eyes, looked up at the morning sky and tried to focus his gaze upon my face. On the right side of his face an ugly purple weal ran from his temple to the cheekbone.

'Water, baas,' he whispered in a voice so faint that I could scarcely make out the words.

There was a gourd floating in the bilge, a cork plug still in its neck. I picked it up and shook it but it was empty. The old man's eyes were closed again; his mouth had fallen open and I could see that his tongue was grey and swollen. A white scum of salt and spittle caked his lips.

At first I was tempted to lift him out of the boat and try to tow him behind me back to the beach, but the tide was against us and I knew the distance was too great.

'Listen to me,' I said to him, 'listen to what I am going to do. I will bail out the canoe and float it again; then I will haul it across the lagoon to the beach. I have plenty of water there.'

The old man made no reply. I slapped him hard across the face.

'Did you hear what I said?' I demanded. 'If you heard me, move your hand. Don't give up your life now. There is plenty of water on the beach.'

I slapped him again, harder this time. He groaned and I saw his hand move in acknowledgement.

I broke the neck off the empty gourd and used it to bail the water from the stern of the canoe in an effort to lighten it sufficiently to slide it off the coral. A few yards from where I stood, the water in the lagoon flowed through the passage like a river in flood; every second that passed lowered the little vessel more firmly into the grip of the coral. I knew that if I left it too late the canoe would be stuck there on top of the reef for another eight hours, until the tide returned to help me float it free. By that time the old man would be beyond help.

There was no time to bail the canoe dry. When I judged

enough water had been removed to allow the vessel to float, I hauled the old man to the stern and propped his head against the wooden seat there. I lifted the rudder out of its retaining rings and threw it in the bottom of the boat; then I waded back to the bows, stooped low in the water and grasped the keel in both hands. There was a muffled splintering of coral beneath the stern post. I felt the little vessel quiver. A lazy swell, larger than its predecessors, broke upon the reef and for a brief moment lifted the canoe from the grip of the coral. I pushed with all my strength; the keel slid reluctantly over the unresisting coral mass and then the canoe was riding free in the deep water on the far side of the reef.

There were no oars in the canoe. I looped the mooring rope at the bows around my chest and drew the vessel behind me through the passage and into the sheltered water of the lagoon. The wind had risen while I was on the reef and by the time I had reached half-way to the beach it began to blow from the island towards the open sea. It caught the canoe broadside and threatened to return it to the reef.

I began to tire; the coarse sisal rope around my chest rode up beneath my arms and chafed the skin. The muscles of my thighs and shoulders throbbed with the unaccustomed effort. I swallowed a mouthful of water and retched miserably. I clung to the bows of the canoe and we drifted slowly back towards the reef. I remember thinking: if I'm not careful, both of us are going to die.

Then, as it does in the middle of most mornings, the wind began to veer into the west. The intolerable weight on the rope eased a little. I forced my arms through the water and we began to move forward again. Slowly and painfully the wavering file of coconut palms along the upper margin of the beach drew closer. The following wind increased in strength and then at last my feet touched the bottom. I stumbled out of the water and hauled the bow of the canoe on to the sand.

The old man was light and fragile as a dessicated reed. I lifted him out of the canoe and carried him up the beach to my shelter. I spread the sleeping bag upon the sand floor and laid him on it. He groaned softly.

'Water, baas,' he whispered. 'You promise me water.'

I uncorked my bottle, full of the cool, crystal water from the lake, and I held it against his lips. He drank greedily, the water spilling over and running down his thin body to melt away into the sand. He tried to speak again but the effort was too much for him. His head fell back against the sleeping bag, his eyes open but unfocused. With the corner of a towel I sponged his injured face, relieved to find the skin unbroken.

I went outside and lit the fire in the hearth. I warmed up the last of the tins of soup. When I took it to him in the shelter he was barely conscious. I held a spoonful of the soup to his mouth and after a while I was able to coax him to drink it.

The warm soup seemed to revive him. He tried to prop himself up on his elbow.

'It was de storm, baas,' he whispered, apparently anxious to explain his presence on the reef. 'I had to chop down de mast.' His head fell back against the blanket I had folded as a pillow for him and instantly he was asleep again.

I left him in the shelter and returned to the canoe. I knocked the bilge plug out of the bottom to drain the water inside; then I made fast the bow rope to a coconut palm at the top of the beach to keep the vessel safe from the grasping fingers of the next high tide. There was nothing more that I could do.

When I returned to the shelter the old man was still asleep. I noticed that his breathing had become more regular and peaceful. I took my mask, snorkel and spear gun from the place I had hung them and walked to the northern end of the beach from where I could approach a stretch of the reef I had not visited before. When he woke up the old man would need food and what was left of my own stocks would never feed us both.

The storm had been followed by an unnatural calm. The grey sediment caught up in the boiling surf had fallen back to its place on the sea floor; beneath the glassy surface of the lagoon there seemed no limit to the distance I could see. The green meadows of the eel grass beds stretched far away; beyond them I could make out the shadow of the reef itself rising from the white sand floor of the lagoon like the sheer wall of a submarine castle. Along the coral battlements the purple banners of the sea fans swayed to the rhythm of the sea.

I dragged the point of my steel arrow through the matrix of an eel grass bed beneath me. As the water cleared, among the emerald blades and the fragments of coral debris I could see the outline of a cerise sea urchin, a pair of lime-green shrimps, a host of frantic worms, a dozen different kinds of mollusc and three small crabs with purple armour and coal-black claws.

I had disturbed the ramparts of a town beneath the sand, a community with its own streets and houses where every inhabitant went about his daily business under constant

108

threat of violent death at the hands of his neighbour.

I watched as all the creatures I had so thoughtlessly uncovered hastened to return to their world of perpetual darkness. The blanket of fine sand I had raised with my spear gun settled back over their homes; in less than a minute all evidence of my intrusion had disappeared. My shadow passed over the place and I swam on.

Not far from that eel grass bed, a stand of elk-horn coral reached up towards the surface. A fat rainbow parrot fish was grazing on one of the flattened coral antlers, low down at the base of the outcrop. My steel arrow passed clean through the polychrome body and gouged a stark white furrow in the coral before it came to rest on the sand.

I turned back towards the beach towing the impaled fish behind me at the end of the arrow's cord. I hauled it out of the water and up the sand. I used my sheath knife to gut the fish there on the beach; as the steel bit into the soft white flesh the brilliant rainbow hues faded and were lost forever.

Over towards the coast of Jamaica I could see the barren white-laced rock that thrust its way out of the sea in the channel between the *cayo* and the mainland. Pale grey streaks of guano ran down its granite flanks to the waterline. The blue haze, which earlier had softened the sharp edge of the horizon, no longer hid it from my view.

High above the lonely rock a living cloud of seagulls wheeled and dived over the water. After my mother left me, I used to think that if I had to return to earth in a different form I should choose to be a gull; and for my home I would select the loneliest pillar of rock that I could find.

When, some months after my mother's departure, my

109

father had brought me to the *cayo* for the first time and I had caught sight of that granite finger pointing to the sky, I had said to myself: that is the exact place; I will be one of those gulls.

Today, I wish that youthful vision of happy solitude still held attractions for me; but it does not.

When I was eighteen I packed a canvas travelling bag, said goodbye to my father and left our Jamaican estate to drift about the coast of Florida, crewing when I could for American yachtsmen and, in the winter, finding work at marinas in Fort Lauderdale or Boca Raton. I carried with me my palette and easel and from time to time I would take a week off to paint the shrimpers along the coast and sell the paintings to anyone who thought them worth a few dollars. Once I camped for a month in the Everglades, struggling to capture on canvas that curious green light which suffuses the cathedral naves beneath the arching branches of the mangroves. I was neither happy nor unhappy during that twilight time as I muddled through the painful transition from boy to man. I relied on no one, sought no favours and made my way entirely on my own.

I was at work in Boca Raton when my father died. He had given no hint in his last letter that he was ill and I was totally unprepared for his death. He was only fifty-three and the telegram said that he had died in his sleep.

I returned to Jamaica for his funeral. At the graveside, I thought how unjust it was that I could feel no true affection for him. After my mother left us and destroyed his life, he had done everything he could to shield me from the worst

110

consequences of her desertion. But it was as if she had taken with her all the affection I was capable of feeling and left none in my soul with which to repay my father for his steadfast, undemonstrative love.

Attached to his Will there was a handwritten note asking me, without much hope I think, to keep the estate within our family where it had been for five generations. But I could never have returned to live in that place of bitter memories and so I sold it. I bought for myself a clapboard bungalow on the north coast of Jamaica, set high on a cliff which overlooked the sea. The paintings of the early period of my career are of the coastline to the east and west of that house, and of the mountains which rise in tiers from the sea to meet the central spine that divides the island. I painted the mountains a lot in those days, enchanted by the subtle, changing light which, after the rain, could bring them so close that I used to feel that I had only to lean over the rail of my verandah to touch them with my brush.

In my own way I was happy there with my paints and canvases and, as more of my paintings found homes overseas and my name became better known, my circle of friends grew wider. Over the years a succession of women passed through that house, but not one of them left more than the faintest trace of her brief passage. I had no intention of ever getting married, and those who knew me best agreed that I was better off alone.

Three months after my father's death, on the day I moved into my new house, I received a letter from my mother. She had married Marcus it seemed; they were living in Trinidad.

Marcus had found a job as Manager of a cocoa estate near Manzanilla. My mother wanted to see me.

'You must have wondered many times how I could have left you when we were so close,' she wrote, and I noticed that the bold strokes of her pen were curiously distorted as if her hand kept creeping up the paper as she formed the letters.

'The truth is that at the time I loved Marcus more than anything else in the world, and so I went away with him. When I sent for you, you wouldn't come. . .'

'Why didn't I say goodbye to you when I left? The truth is that, because I loved you, I couldn't bear to see your pain. . .'

There was more than three pages of it, every paragraph proclaiming the truth as she saw it, every page explaining, correcting, justifying. But the final words were quite different. They were written in the form of a postscript, huddled down at the foot of the last page, crabbed and almost illegible as if the letters had been formed with great effort. The postscript read simply:

'Please forgive.'

I remember how I folded the letter in half, taking care to see that all the edges lined up beneath each other; then I tore it into small pieces. The wind lifted them from my palm and carried them down the face of the cliff to the open sea below my house. I watched as they drifted out on the ebbing tide.

When I did not reply to that letter it was followed by another and another and then still more, all written in exactly the same words. After a while I stopped opening them; at last the flow slackened and then ceased altogether.

I told myself that I was pleased with the way I had reacted to those letters. The old *houngan* had predicted that I would be a prideful man; and proud men, after all, do not forgive the unforgivable.

Some five years after that spate of letters from my mother came to an end, a visitor called at my house. He was a courteous old man with a neatly trimmed beard and a mane of grizzled hair, and when I failed to recognise him he introduced himself as Marcus, my mother's second husband.

I did not take his hand, but we went inside and sat together on the verandah overlooking the sea. There was a regatta in progress at the time, I remember, and the horizon was studded with the bone-white sails and rainbow spinnakers of the yachts out of Montego Bay.

In the months which had followed my mother's departure from our estate, I thought a lot about Marcus. There was one particular fantasy which had pleased me more than the others. In it I captured him, bent together the tops of two young palm trees and bound one of his arms to the crown of each tree. When the moment suited me I allowed the palms to spring apart, in just the way that old Sinis the Pine Bender had served unwary travellers in my cloth-bound copy of *Tales of Troy and Greece*.

I used to keep Marcus waiting a long time for death in those days. Cutlass in hand, I would crouch over the rope which held the trees together while I recited for all the world to hear the catalogue of his treachery.

I developed more than one version of how Marcus behaved in this predicament, but in my favourite fantasy he whimpered like a weak-kneed woman, begging vainly for forgiveness from his perch between the palm trees until, finally, I tired of him and severed the retaining rope with one swift stroke of the cutlass.

'I never forgive,' I used to shout at the top of my voice as the cutlass fell in a bright arc upon the tensioned rope.

I had once read accounts of the suppression of the Indian Mutiny. In them was a vivid description of how the captured mutineers were fired from the mouth of cannon at Cawn-pore, and how, after the discharge of the guns, only their arms remained still roped to the wheels of the gun carriages. In my imagination Marcus suffered a similar fate: only his arms could be found after the trees had sprung apart, one attached to the crown of each palm. Above the site of the execution the chicken hawks wheeled in tight circles, gathering to dispose of the scattered remains.

On the verandah of my house, his arms now firmly attached to his shoulders, Marcus said in his curiously gentle voice: 'I have come to tell you that your mother died last week. I am very sorry to disturb you, but she wanted me to bring you the news personally. She made me promise before she went.'

He looked out across the lapis lazuli surface of the bay towards the sail-studded rim of the horizon, enveloped now in a fine blue haze of heat. I noticed for the first time that his eyes were red and watery, the eyelids unnaturally swollen.

'She was very unhappy with your father, you know,' he said quietly. 'Sometimes, when they're unhappy, people do things which they live to regret.'

He shifted his gaze and looked closely at me in the brilliant light of the afternoon sun, shading his bloodshot eyes with the palm of his hand.

'You have grown to look much like her,' he said. 'I am sorry she never saw you after you grew up.'

I thought then that he was going to scold me, to say that I could have spared her so much unhappiness by responding to her letters. I braced myself to make a cold retort, because I would not be lectured by the man who had taken her away from me; but he did nothing of the kind. He merely finished the drink I had poured for him, stood up and thanked me with old-fashioned courtesy for receiving him.

'She suffered a great deal these past five years,' he said on the doorstep. 'She tried to disguise it, but it showed in ways she could not conceal.'

I thought at once of the strangely distorted writing I had noticed in that first letter. Then Marcus was gone.

Afterwards, I scrambled down the steep path which had been carved into the face of the limestone cliff to the deserted beach beneath it. As I kicked viciously at the flotsam along the water's edge there were only two thoughts in my mind: that Marcus must be grieving too, and I had offered him no word of sympathy; and that it would not have cost me my life to have written just once to my mother and said simply: 'It is all right; I understand.'

By next morning, however, that sombre mood had passed.

Two days after Marcus's visit I returned to the estate where I was born. I had deliberately kept well away from the place since my father's death, but now I wanted to see it again, to bring back life for a few hours to the memories of my mother and my childhood in that sprawling house among the fields of sugar cane.

It was a three-hour journey over the mountains to the opposite side of the island. As I turned off the main road on to the unpaved driveway which led through the fields to the house, I saw that the tall metal gates which once guarded the entrance to our property had fallen from their hinges; they lay rusting in the long grass. On the other side of the road an ancient black man squatted in the shade of a mango tree, idly watching his herd of goats gorge themselves on the rotting yellow fruit. I parked my car and walked over to him. He accepted a cigarette and I asked why the fallen gates had not been replaced.

'Well, baas,' he said, collecting his thoughts with difficulty, 'dere ain't no need. No one live dere any more.' He took a deep pull at the cigarette. 'Fact is, dere ain't no purpose fixin' de gates now, 'cause dey don' protect nothin' no more.'

I left him smoking his cigarette and drove on cautiously between the leaning gate posts and up the pot-holed road towards the house. Half a mile further on the encroaching bush finally narrowed the road to a rough track. I got out of the car and walked. Thick blades of razor-edged guinea grass invaded the path and it was clear that no one had been that way for a long time. I remembered how carefully the drive had been maintained when I was a boy and what pride my father had taken in the palm-lined approach to our house. It was difficult to believe now that the road had ever been anything more than an overgrown goat track.

The mid-morning sun burned in a cloudless sky and all

around me shimmering waves of heat rose from the bone-dry grass. The fields on either side of the path, once green and fertile with sugar cane, had long since been reclaimed by the bush. In a few isolated places a sickly cane stalk struggled above the level of the grass, but the orange trees my father had planted in the intervals between the fields had been choked by the invading undergrowth; their twisted trunks lay full length on the ground.

The path began to scale a low rise at the top of which had stood the estate Barracks. The Barracks had been a long, palm-thatched wooden building which housed the families of those labourers with nowhere else to live. Whenever I rode my donkey that way, the smell of boiling fish and green bananas used to greet me long before the decrepit building came in sight; and in the evenings I would see the women squatting on the steps of the building like so many chattering blackbirds, taking it in turns to plait each other's woolly hair. They used to pause at my approach and raise their hands in greeting.

There was no water tank near the Barracks, so twice each day the children were despatched on a scramble down the steep path to a shallow pool in an arm of the river which bisected our estate. Each journey took more than an hour and sometimes I would meet the children staggering up the hill on their return from the river, their black faces contorted with the effort of balancing a five-gallon kerosene tin full of water on their small round heads.

Once, I remember, a child stumbled on the rocky path just as he reached the top of the hill and the precious load of water cascaded on to the dry earth. He was a boy of about my own age, dirty and undernourished, dressed only in a pair of khaki shorts. He looked first at the empty tin lying on the ground and then back at the steep path which he knew he would have to climb all over again; and then he looked at me, the son of the white master of the estate, with my clean shirt and polished boots, and I knew exactly what he was thinking. I had a sudden yearning to say something which would bridge the gulf between us, but he grabbed the empty tin and turned his back on me before I could speak. I watched his small figure retreating down the path towards the river, defiantly swinging the kerosene tin over his head and muttering something to himself which I could not hear.

When I reached the top of the rise I could find no trace of the Barracks beneath the galba trees whose branches had once formed a canopy above it. On the level ground below me, however, I saw that the pale scar of the driveway was still there, but it had been swamped by an invading tangle of vines and wild guava trees. The vines were hung with delicate, bell-shaped purple flowers and I saw that they were wilting in the fierce heat of the morning sun.

I could remember vividly how the approach to the house had looked when I was a boy. For the final furlong, before the drive curved round to meet the broad front steps of the house, the roadway was flanked by a splendid double row of royal palms. The smooth grey trunks soared straight upwards for more than a hundred and fifty feet like the columns of some ruined tropical temple, bursting at the top into dark green circlets of feathery leaves. Now there were ugly gaps, like missing teeth, in the elegant row of palms.

At the far end of the avenue the site of the house was still marked by a wide circle of poinciana trees. They, too, were in bloom and their scarlet flowers made a great blaze of colour in that encroaching sea of green; but the house itself had vanished. A few truncated pillars still remained, but they were curiously distorted and patterned by swirling black stains. The building had been destroyed by fire and, judging by the size of the young poincianas which had taken root inside the ruined walls, it had all happened a long time ago.

In a few more years, I thought, the surviving pillars would collapse in their turn and only the circle of poincianas and the gap-toothed avenue of palms would be left to mark the site of the place where I was born. Perhaps in the years to come other people would rediscover the ruins, just as I had stumbled upon the ruins of the Indian settlement in the mud of the little stream at the bottom of the rose garden.

I returned the way I had come. Beside the fallen gates at the entrance to the property the old man was still keeping watch over his goats.

'What happened to the people who owned the estate?' I asked him.

'I don' exactly know what happen to dem, baas,' he replied. 'But I hear say dey couldn' live togedder in peace. It seem dat dey was a heartless people. . . It was a pity really, 'cause dat family own de land for near on two hundred years.'

My question had been about the family to whom I had sold the estate on my father's death; with a bitter sense of shock I realised that the old man was referring to us, to my family, and that was how he saw us.

'You have any more cigarettes, baas?' he wheedled.

I gave him the packet. Then I turned my back on the fallen gates and all the memories of my childhood. As I climbed into the car for the long drive home, I had been furious to discover that for the first time in many years my face was wet with tears.

The old fisherman was awake when I returned to the shelter bearing the parrotfish wrapped in a sea grape leaf. He greeted me quietly and I thought that he looked stronger after his long sleep. I roasted the fish on the stone hearth and the old man ate it together with the soft heart of a breadfruit.

When evening came he crawled out of the shelter and together we walked slowly through the grove of coconut palms to the beach. He did not need my arm. We sat on the warm sand above the line of the high tide and I produced what remained of the brandy. In companionable silence we watched the purple glow above the western horizon give place to the velvet darkness of the Caribbean night. The first stars appeared as trembling pin points of amber light in the blue-black vault of the sky. There was no moon.

I passed the bottle to the old man. We looked out into the darkness to where the presence of the reef was marked by a thin white crescent stitched to the surface of the water.

'It is a clear night,' I said, in order to break the silence between us.

'Yes,' said the old man. 'Dere will be no rain.'

'Where do you come from?' I asked.

He named a village on the south coast of Jamaica. I had been there only once but I retained an impression of a picturesque cluster of red-roofed huts perched above a horseshoe bay. I had thought of returning to paint the scene, but I never did.

'Are you content there?' I asked.

He looked out into the darkness again. 'You know, baas,' he said softly, 'God never give me money nor a big house like some people; but he give me dat place to live in, an' he give me eyes to see dat it is beautiful.'

He took a deep pull at the brandy. 'I don' believe a man have a right to expect more from life dan dat.'

I nodded my agreement, surprised to find that a poetic soul lived behind that seamed black face.

'Tell me about the storm,' I said. 'How is it that you were not fishing with a partner?'

'I had a partner wid me,' he replied quietly. 'It was my son.'

I thought: my God, the old man's lost his son. But I was wrong.

'When de storm catch us,' he continued before I could speak, 'we was both fishing close togedder. De sea was very bad already, tall waves an' plenty rain. Den de wind rise up sudden. I take it for a squall, only it never pass over. My son haul down his sail in good time. He call to me: "Papa, haul down you sail." But de rope was frayed an' it jam in de pully. I could not move it.'

He took another long pull at the brandy as the memory of that moment returned in all its urgency.

'I let de sail fly out, but de wind catch it an' de boat heel over. Water rush in over de stern. I take up de cutlass from the bilge an' I chop down de mast. As it fall it strike me 'pon de head.'

121

He raised his hand to his wounded temple. In the darkness I could just make out the fingers of his other hand clenching and unclenching in his lap.

'I call out to my son to take me up,' he continued, 'but I could see dat fear catch hold of him. He had a mind den only to save himself.'

He returned to the bottle of brandy to fortify himself against the memory.

'What happened then?' I prompted.

'De wind back into de north an' ease a little. I see him raise his sail again; den he haul roun' de tiller of his canoe an' he set course back to de mainland.'

'He left you there to drown?' I asked incredulously.

The old man nodded. 'Yes,' he said simply. 'But it was not my time yet. I take up de calabash an' I manage to bail out some of de water. After dat I mus' have faint from de blow on de head. De current catch hold of de canoe an' in de mornin' you fin' me on de reef.'

I got up and walked slowly back to the shelter to light the fire in the hearth. I shifted the four corner stones about for no good reason and stacked more neatly the pile of driftwood on the sand beside them.

When I returned to the beach I saw that the old man had not moved. His eyes were focused on the invisible horizon; he was looking out through the darkness towards the place where he had been left to drown by his own son. I put my hand on his shoulder in an awkward gesture of comfort.

Together we finished the rest of the brandy and I buried the empty bottle deep in the sand.

'When you get back to your village,' I asked, 'what will

you do about your son?'

The question seemed to perplex him.

'Do about him, baas?' he asked. 'How you mean, do about him?'

'Well,' I said, beginning to regret that I had raised the question, 'you can't pretend that it never happened. No one can just forgive a man who behaves like that.'

'Forgive him?' the old man replied. 'But of course I forgive him.'

'But he left you to drown,' I said bluntly.

He was plainly astonished.

'You forgettin' somethin', baas; we human bein's, we are frail creatures. We fall easy to temptation; it is in our nature.'

I said nothing.

'You know what de Galilean taught: forgive us our sins as we forgive those who sin against us. We mus' learn to pardon each other. Dere is no other way.'

He looked closely at me in the darkness.

'You have no sins, baas?' he asked.

I did not answer his question.

'I don't believe in God,' I said.

'Dat don' make no difference,' he replied at once. 'You don' have to believe to see de sense in it.'

He had been lying on his back in the sand; now he sat upright beside me.

'In our bodies we human bein's are no different from de animals,' he said, groping for the words to convey what he clearly felt so deeply. 'But unlike dem we have de power to love – an' dat means we have de power to forgive. If I don' use dat power, den I remain on a level wid de animals; in fact

123

I am lower, because I have de freedom to choose. Dat is why I forgive my son.'

'But what about your pride?' I demanded.

'I have no pride,' he said simply. 'It was a weight aroun' my neck an' I put it aside long ago.'

'Well, I am proud,' I said defiantly.

'Den, baas, I have to tell you dat you are de less because of it,' the old man replied.

I had nothing to say after that, and it was clear that he too had nothing more to say. He was a taciturn old man really, and it was only the brandy that had loosened his tongue. I had the feeling that he wished he had kept his silence since it was apparent that I could not understand; but in a curious fashion even then we were not uncomfortable in each other's company.

After a while he was ready for sleep. He stood up, courteously wished me goodnight and retired to the shelter. Through the palm-thatch wall I could hear him arranging the blanket beneath his head; he belched softly in the darkness, turned over and almost immediately he was asleep.

Sleep eluded me. I sprawled beside the driftwood fire watching the shadows of the palm trees dance upon the sand. The shrill song of a distant cicada and the soft gasp of the waves along the beach gave voice to the night.

My thoughts kept returning to the old fisherman.

'Forgive him?' he had repeated, astonished by my question. 'But of course I forgive him. . .'

And then: 'We are frail creatures, we human beings. We

124

fall easy to temptation; it is in our nature. . .'

I looked out through the darkness to the pale white crescent of the reef. I was glad that chance had placed the *cayo* in the path of the old man's waterlogged canoe. I did not like the thought of him lying helpless in his dismasted vessel with the sharks of the Gulf Stream gathering impatiently around him. Then I remembered that only four days earlier I had cursed the same blind chance for setting down the island across the drifting route of a colony of purple sea snails.

I must have fallen asleep at that point, for out of the circle of light cast by the fire, forming and dissolving like mist over the lake, I thought I saw Simone's face, those cornflower eyes jewelled by tears.

'Forgive me, darling,' she kept saying, 'forgive me. . .'

I shook myself awake and threw a bamboo log upon the dying fire. A thin column of sparks flew up into the darkness. From somewhere beyond the grove of palm trees a nightjar whistled its plaintive, high-pitched call.

'You have no sins, baas?' the old man had asked.

Against my will my thoughts turned to the women I had used so shamefully and then discarded in the days before I met Simone. Had any of them forgiven me, I wondered.

I turned my back to the light of the fire and groped through the morass of my new uncertainty towards the merciful release of sleep.

Sunday, June 25th

I woke while it was still dark this morning convinced that I was dead. Someone had been writing about me. I leant over his shoulder to read the words.

'They found him face down,' I read, 'not far from the place where he had built his shelter. The drifting sand and the fallen leaves had already begun to cover his body; the fabric of the island was reaching out to embrace him in death.

'They dug a grave and laid his body within it. They left no mark over the place where he was buried and by next morning the wind had erased the evidence of their spades; and so he was united forever with the body of the island he loved.

'But for those people for whom he could find no forgiveness in his heart, it was as if he had never existed. . .'

I believe that I was yelling at the top of my voice when I woke up, repeating over and over again: 'I don't want that, I don't want that. . .'

The noise disturbed the old man in the shelter. He crawled out, rubbing the sleep from his eyes with the back of his hand, his face a dark mask in the moonlight.

He stood beside me on the sand and placed a hand on my shoulder.

'Is all right, baas,' he said in his soft voice, 'I am here wid you. No one can trouble you now. Go back to sleep.'

'Yes,' I said thickly, struggling to free myself from the grip of the nightmare, 'it was only a dream.'

Comforted by his presence I lay down on the sand again and the nightmare did not return.

When I awoke for the second time this morning the sun was high above the horizon, the diamond light filtering through the palm fronds above me and playing across my face.

Down at the water's edge I could see the old fisherman working on his canoe. From the bamboo grove at the foot of the hill he had cut a new mast and he was already bending on to it the spare canvas sail from the bow locker. He had hammered the bilge plug back into place and the scarred rudder lay on the sand waiting to be slipped into its retaining rings on the sternpost as soon as the canoe was launched.

Beyond the crescent reef the swell was gentle. A band of cloud which overhung the western horizon marked the position beneath it of the Jamaican mainland. A fresh breeze blew across the approach to the Windward Passage from the direction of Haiti. With the wind behind him it would not take long to get home.

I walked across the sand to the canoe.

'I glad you wake up, baas,' the old man said. 'I goin' leave now an' I want to t'ank you for what you done for me. I will not forget you.'

He hesitated; I sensed that he wished to add something else but did not want to offend me.

'I hear you cry out in de night,' he said at last. 'I not askin' about your private business, but I believe only a woman can trouble a man like dat. Remember, it is like I say last night: we are all frail vessels, we human beins; an' if life teach me one t'ing it is dat we must lift up each other when we fall.'

I made no reply but helped him in silence to heave the canoe down the slope of the beach and back into the sea. It rode high on the even surface of the water, as light and graceful in its proper element as it had been clumsy and lopsided on the sand. I fitted the rudder into its retaining rings.

The old man raised the mast with the sail attached and at once the breeze caught the rust-stained canvas and bore the canoe across the lagoon and out through the passage in the coral. He turned on his seat in the stern, one hand laid firmly about the tiller; he raised the other hand in brief salute. I watched from where I stood at the water's edge as the stained triangle of sail grew smaller and smaller until I could no longer distinguish it with certainty from the white horses that flecked the tumbled surface of the open sea.

A black-headed laughing gull, which had followed the canoe from the *cayo* in the vain hope of a gift of fish, turned back to the island in disappointment. The bird passed low over my head on its way to the nesting sites above the cliff face that overlooked the windward shore.

That sense of uncertainty and desolation, which only two days earlier had clawed at my heart, returned to rack me again. I wandered aimlessly about the *cayo*, blind for once to the changing colours on the face of the lagoon and to the falling blossom of the poincianas which dropped like scarlet snow upon the sand.

Thirty years ago an old woman with a face like a crumpled leaf had spread the bloody intestines of a chicken upon the earth and declared that I would grow up to be an unforgiving man. At night, in the castle of my bedroom, for months after that journey up the mountain, I used to whisper to myself above the chorus of the bullfrogs in the stream: I am proud; I am going to be hard; I will not be hurt again. And gradually, as I grew older, that dark image of myself became reality and I assumed the form the old *houngan* had predicted.

Now an ancient black fisherman, cast upon me by a storm and some freak vagary of the current, had sowed doubt in my mind where before there had been only certainty and bitter resolve.

'We are frail creatures, we human beings,' he had said. 'We must lift each other up when we fall.'

I sat on the edge of the cliff overlooking the wild, tumbled windward shore and all afternoon the words echoed and re-echoed in the troubled cavern of my mind. Two hundred feet beneath me a long Atlantic swell reared up like a prancing stallion and shattered itself against the bulwark of granite boulders. The sun struck rainbows in the flying spray.

'My God,' I whispered, 'that is beautiful. . .' I watched as the spray fell back to the water, and through it, dimly as through a glittering silver curtain, I saw for the first time that there might be beauty in more than those material objects whose form and colour could be captured on a canvas, like the arc of a wave or the pattern on the shell of a cowry. I saw that there could be beauty, too, in less substantial things, in the love of one human being for another, in a deed of

129

compassion, and even – was it possible? – in an act of for-giveness.

I thought about myself and about the old fisherman. Both of us had been wounded by people we loved: by to-morrow night both of us would be back on the mainland. But while he was returning to the joy of reconciliation, I should be coming back to the bleak world of lawyers and divorce courts and the dismantling of the framework of my life.

I lost all sense of time there on the edge of the cliff. Deliberately, I kept my back to the sunset and when at last I returned to my shelter the night was black as pitch and I had to make use of the trunks of the coconut palms to guide me to the place.

My sleep was full of wild shapes and voices that drifted in and out of a timeless, swirling mist. Only the placid, moonlit eyes of the old fisherman seemed real, and in my dream he beckoned me to follow him out of the mist to a brighter place whose tall gates I could just make out in the distance behind him.

But I refused to leave the familiar world of the mist and after a while he went away and did not return.

Monday, June 26th

The canoe came into sight on the western horizon just before mid-day. I demolished the little palm-thatched shelter in which I had lived and removed the fire-blackened stones that formed the rectangle of my hearth. I returned the bamboo supports to the place where I had found them on the beach and scattered the coconut boughs beneath the trees around me. I cut a branch from the almond tree and swept the place on which the shelter had stood until the sand was smooth again and nothing remained to suggest that the shelter had existed.

I was determined to leave no evidence of my brief sojourn on the island. I had found it unblemished and I wanted to leave it that way. The *cayo* was a setting made for love and happiness; it did not deserve me with my troubled dreams. If it possessed a soul of its own, as the Indians believed, then it would see me depart without sorrow.

I watched from the beach as the canoe tacked to pass through the passage in the reef; the man at the tiller hauled in his trolling line. The tar-stained vessel cut a spreading furrow across the polished surface of the lagoon; then the sail was drawn down and the keel grated on the sand in front of me.

The two fishermen greeted me cheerfully, relieved I think to find I was still sane. One of them took up my canvas bag and stowed it in the canoe. I climbed into the vessel, the sail was hoisted and with the wind behind us we slipped easily through the passage in the coral and out on to the open sea.

Above us a flock of pelicans in arrow head formation kept station with the canoe. As the island fell swiftly astern they circled once and then returned to their home on the lagoon. A part of me, I thought, went with them and would lodge there forever.

The canoe made good time over the long, restless swell; the wind stayed firmly in the east and filled out the threadbare sail. The man in the bows fell asleep, just as he had done on the outward journey, his chin propped against the rough planks of the bow locker. The sour stench of stale marijuana clung to his clothes. The helmsman baited his trolling line, tossed the baited hook over the stern and hummed softly to himself the plaintive chorus of an old Jamaican mento. For the last time I watched the silhouette of the little island tremble on the lip of the horizon and then fall away out of my sight.

I turned on my damp, uncomfortable seat to face the mainland, clearly visible now in the blue haze ahead of us. At that moment the helmsman remembered something he had brought for me. He reached into the locker beneath his seat and drew out a creased white envelope.

'I nearly forget, baas,' he said casually. 'A lady give me dis for you jus' as we leave dis mornin'. I believe she waitin' at de hotel for you.'

The writing on the envelope was Simone's. The ink had been smudged and the last three letters of my name were illegible. That locker isn't watertight, I remember thinking

132

foolishly. Then the blood rushed to my face and my heart threatened to burst the confines of my chest.

On a sheet of pale blue notepaper bearing the name of the small hotel that overlooked the harbour for which we were heading, she had written:

'Darling – Please forgive.'

That was all. She had not put her name to the letter; in the past when we wrote to each other neither of us ever did. It was understood in those days that there could be no one else in our lives.

I do not know for how long I sat there vacant eyed in the swaying canoe, the letter crushed between my fingers. I was conscious at last of the curious gaze of the helmsman.

'I hope it is not bad news, baas,' he inquired solicitously.

I shook my head and folded the letter carefully in half and then in half again. I tore it into small pieces and I let the wind carry them out of my hand and scatter them over the surface of the sea behind us. I watched them dance briefly in the white-flecked wake and then they were lost. It was in just that way, I reflected, that I had disposed of the letters my mother had once written to me.

The day which had begun so brightly on the *cayo* became increasingly overcast with the approach of evening. As we tacked through the mouth of the little harbour, however, the clouds which hung over the mountains lifted and a broad shaft of sunlight fell across the bay. But the sunshine was short lived. The band of cloud returned and a curtain of mist rolled down towards the sea. A thin drizzle welcomed me back to the Jamaican mainland.

We ran alongside the same frail wooden jetty from which we had left eight days earlier. I paid off the fishermen. We shook hands and I carried my canvas bag across the open square to where I had left my car in the shadow of the peeling customs shed. In the dust which had settled on the bonnet of the car some idle hand had drawn a giant phallus; the words beneath it were pock-marked by the drizzle. I struck through them with the flat of my hand and stowed my bag on the back seat.

I slipped behind the wheel and turned the key in the ignition; the engine coughed but did not start first time. I sat there in the driver's seat, my fingers curled around the key, and I looked up at the mountain which overhung the village. It was curiously flattened at the top, like that other mountain behind our estate where I had first seen the old woman crouched like a withered monkey at the back of her *tonnelle*. In my mind's eye, I saw her spread the chicken entrails once again over the hard-packed earthern floor, saw how the way they fell determined the kind of man that I would be. The stench of blood was strong in my nostrils.

Then the seamed face of the old fisherman was imposed upon the image of the *houngan* and I could no longer see the chicken entrails or the floor of the *tonnelle*. Broad rivulets of sweat ran down my temples; the *houngan*'s hoarse monotone echoed in my ears.

Something gave way deep within me.

'God damn you, old witch,' I heard myself shout. 'To hell with your bogus prophecy.'

134

A small black boy who was turning cartwheels at the edge of the open square looked round at me in gap-toothed astonishment; there was no one else about.

I climbed out of the car and started the long walk up the hill behind the village, following the narrow, pot-holed road which led to the hotel, defeated at last.

I walked slowly up the hill, deliberately dragging my feet through the iron-grey dust, reluctant still to say goodbye to that hard image of myself, so carefully nurtured over all those years.

Twice I stopped at the edge of the road to look down upon the bay, and on each occasion my pride fought to turn me back. On the eastern horizon the sky had cleared and the setting sun lit up a pillar of cloud suspended high above the water. Beneath it, I knew, lay my *cayo*. For all my efforts to remove every sign of my brief occupation, some traces still remained. My footprints still led from the site of my shelter to the point on the beach where I had boarded the canoe.

In due course the wind and the rain and the nocturnal wanderings of the ghost crabs would obliterate them; but not yet, please God, I prayed, not just yet.

From the verandah of the clapboard hotel she saw me climbing the hill. She ran down the steep slope to meet me. In the failing light I saw the comet's tail of her red-gold hair streaming out behind her, just as I had seen it on the day we met.

As I gathered her into my arms I heard myself say: 'I want to tell you. . .', and there in the dust at the edge of the pitted road I told her for the first time about my mother and about my visit to the *houngan* and why it was that I wore a kind of armour round my heart. And I told her, too, about the old fisherman who had taught me that we must lift up each other when we fall.

And finally I told her how I loved her; and once the barrier had been lifted those pent-up, unfamiliar words of love tripped and stumbled over each other in their haste until at last she stopped the torrent with her lips.

In the moment of silence that fell between us as I returned her kiss, I felt the brittle carapace of my spurious pride crumble and fall about me like a worn-out suit of armour. For the first time in thirty years I was defenceless; but to my surprise there was no pain, no pain at all.